VONNA HARPER

Dark Touch

ELLORA'S CAVE
ROMANTICA® PUBLISHING

What the critics are saying...

୪

"Dark and unsettling, yet the love scenes Mace and Sara share are emotional and strangely arusing. A paranormal aspect and an unusually interesting storyline." ~ *Sizzling Romance*

"Not a story for the faint of heart [...] really pulls you into the characters and gies you an in-depth mentale picture of what it's like to be them [...] a dark tale of domination and submission and how love can overcome both." ~ *Just Erotic Romance Reviews*

An Ellora's Cave Romantica Publication

www.ellorascave.com

Dark Touch

ISBN 9781419951176
ALL RIGHTS RESERVED.
Dark Touch Copyright © 2004 Vonna Harper
Edited by Martha Punches.
Cover art by Syneca.

This book printed in the U.S.A. by Jasmine-Jade Enterprises, LLC.

Electronic book Publication June 2004
Trade paperback Publication September 2005

Excerpt from *Hard Bodies* Copyright © Vonna Harper, 2002

Also by Vonna Harper

&

About the Author

❧

Under her "real" name, Vonna Harper has published more fiction than she can keep track of. These include category romances for the major players as well as the 'juicy' stuff. She also penned a series of well-received Native American historicals. One earned her finalist status in both the Women Writing the West Willa award and Pacific Northwest Booksellers Association. Before discovering romances, both erotic and otherwise, Vonna 'confessed' all kinds of nonsense for the confession magazines.

When asked about erotica research, she insists, "Of course I've time-traveled to the ancient Everglades, infiltrated bondage strongholds, done wilderness search and rescue, and spent a night trapped in a workout gym with Mr. Universe. How can I possibly write about something I haven't experienced?"

As for day jobs, "I've been a commercial pilot, brain surgeon, worked as a white-water river guide, bee keeper, snake charmer, and garbage collector."

And if you buy all that, she'd like you to check out the bridge she has listed on eBay.

Vonna welcomes comments from readers. You can find her website and email address on her author bio page at www.ellorascave.com.

Tell Us What You Think

We appreciate hearing reader opinions about our books. You can email us at Comments@EllorasCave.com.

DARK TOUCH

Prologue

ജ

Something — something dark.

The *outsider's* flesh felt hot and cold. Bodies pressed against her and held her prisoner. Panic nipped at her nerve endings, and she fought for control. Bodies surrounded her like a living wall. Another breath, deeper than the first, brought no relief. She tasted cigarette smoke and smelled human flesh. It didn't matter that she'd been here before. Knowing what was coming only increased her apprehension.

Escape! By shoving against a massive side, she forced enough space so she could turn around. Shadows like blackened ocean waves washed over her until she felt as if she was drowning. The walls were decorated with neon beer signs, and light from them slapped ineffectively at the night with thin red flashes that cast sober faces in eerie hues. Why was she here again? How —

A sound as wavelike as the shadows distracted her. The sound grew quickly, held at an awful pitch, then fell away. When it was back to a level that allowed thought, she slid forward until a man with a back so wide she couldn't have spanned it with her outstretched arms stopped her. He lifted a foaming mug to his lips and drank repeatedly. The men flanking him did the same.

A new voice, young and female, cut through the hard riding buzz. The sound was quickly followed by a horribly familiar masculine bellow that threatened to bury the *outsider* in memories of forced, violent, on-the-edge sex. The young female spoke again, her tone sharp and trimmed with fear.

Someone bumped into the *outsider*, knocking her off-balance. She fought to right herself and looked around. The beer signs still flung their whimsical lights. If this was a battle between color and night, the night was winning.

The young female sobbed, sounding like an injured child, but the hornet's nest of voices and music never slackened. Hadn't anyone else heard? Surely —

A scream this time.

"Help her!" the *outsider* yelled. "Can't you —"

But there was no one, only expanding bodies. Frantic, the *outsider* pushed and elbowed and clawed until she found an opening in the mountains of flesh. She lurched forward until she ran into an empty stool and righted herself by grabbing a bar blemished by sticky globs. She caught sight of a fractured reflection and realized she was looking at herself in a broken mirror that stretched the length of the bar.

Her face with its long, tangled hair and eyes like spots of midnight on a too-white canvas buckled and waved and faded.

Then the mist was no more. Instead, two figures were now superimposed on the mirror that couldn't be one after all because the wall behind it no longer existed.

The *outsider* glanced down. The wooden floor had turned into dusty, oil-spattered gravel.

The figures became clearer, so sharply defined now that the *outsider* could make out a female's slender body and a man's larger, threatening one. The young female backed away, hands up but no more effective against the man's blows than apple blossoms in a storm.

"Help her! Someone, please, help her!"

Again and again the man struck the midnight-eyed female's face and neck and body. Her screams shattered like fine glass, and her arms hung at her side. The fingers of her right hand were curled around something. "Help me. Please, help me," she sobbed.

"How?" the *outsider* asked. "I don't know what to do." *I didn't when I was on the receiving end.*

The young female's hand came up; light touched the knife she held.

The attacker closed in on his victim, heavy boots crunching on gravel. His face remained in shadow, but the *outsider* felt as if she was being ripped apart by his unseen eyes. Felt the familiar power of his approaching body.

His fury.

His hatred, power, and control she knew all too well.

Sobbing, Sara Parmenter dug her nails into her pillow. Still fighting to free herself from the quicksand inside her mind, she rolled onto her back and surged upright. Night air lapped at her shoulders but didn't cool her sweat. She sucked in air, smelling sage and old wood. The clean scents cleaned her lungs of the cigarette smoke that had been a powerful part of the nightmare.

"Not again," she whimpered. "Please, not again!"

Chapter One

ဢ

The mix of flute and hand-harp filled the black sport car's interior. Mace Seeger rolled down the window so he could smell the sweet, dry sage growing everywhere and fading into the thin, distant crack between sky and earth, which was almost all this part of eastern Oregon had to offer. He imagined the music from his tape flowing out over the land until it slipped off into some shadowless place. It seemed fitting to be listening to a Hopi rain chant while driving through high prairie country, peaceful when he desperately needed that. Music also helped blunt the car's aura of power and rage—echoes of its dead owner.

He'd been driving since late yesterday because after six months, he could no longer fight the demands inside his fractured mind and body. Against all sanity, and even the chance of getting stopped by the police, he'd gotten into Ronnie Parmenter's car and headed north with not so much as a change of clothes and precious little cash. The moon had already muted the night when he left California and entered Oregon. He'd been impressed by the swath I-5 cut through the mountains, but last night he'd seen little of hard peaks and Mt. Shasta's veil of snow. He should have spent the night in the quaint town of Ashland and gone for an early morning walk in the large, lush and peaceful park there. But something more powerful than the need for rest had driven him on.

When a pickup passed him on the lonely highway that now wandered east, he returned the cowboy hat-wearing driver's wave, then fast-forwarded to change tape sides. In the past half hour he'd seen maybe three other vehicles, two farms, and a lean woman on horseback with a couple of dogs trotting behind as she headed toward some cattle. The truck driver and horsewoman belonged here the same as the antelope, buzzards, and jackrabbits.

As for him—as for him what?

Acknowledging that logic means little to a man pushed by regret and self-recrimination brought a brief, mirthless smile to his lips. He'd prefer to believe his mind had splintered because he'd been without sleep for nearly forty-eight hours, but sleep deprivation, like an insanity plea, wasn't the truth.

What was? Certainly it couldn't be that he'd carried a photograph of a naked and tied woman in his wallet and mind for so long that she'd taken over his soul. Neither could it be the look in her eyes—fearful, angry, proud and wild despite the bonds.

A cramped muscle in his instep distracted him. He took his foot off the gas and flexed his toes until the pain subsided. By then he was traveling at little more than twenty miles an hour. If he continued at that speed, he might never reach the address on Ronnie Parmenter's driver's license, a place he had no business going to.

Still, he accelerated until the wind coming through the open window raked his flesh and cooled a little of his reaction to the photograph. He tried humming along with the tape, but the piece was a collection of desert sounds. There was little rhythm to wolf howls and frog croaks. He couldn't remember how long ago he'd eaten and wondered if that might have something to do with his inability to explain what the hell he was doing.

Maybe the car should smell of leather and cigarette smoke as it had when he'd first forced himself behind the wheel, but that had been six months ago. Now its scent put him in mind of dust and disuse. If he'd been thinking, he would have changed the oil and checked the spark plugs.

Thinking had nothing to do with why he was hundreds of miles from home when he should be in the Sutter County almond orchards he managed.

He considered what life would be like if he was a gypsy with no agenda other than seeing where tires and metal took him. The question of how he would support himself came up, but this was his fantasy. He'd deal with logic later.

Just as he'd deal with what he'd say to Ronnie Parmenter's widow when he saw her.

Saw her? Put a voice and flesh to the helpless sex slave she'd once been?

His eyes were stinging from the sandpaper behind his lids when it dawned on him that there was something different about the nearly treeless land. He was looking at barbed wire fence. He couldn't see any cattle, but they might be grazing in one of the many draws. One thing about being responsible for almond trees, they remained where they'd been planted.

Armed with that piece of wisdom, he rubbed away what he could of the sandpaper and made out several distant bumps that might be buildings. Prineville wasn't that far away, but because there weren't any signs of the central Oregon town out here, it was all too easy to imagine the farm being the proverbial million miles from nowhere.

The dots slowly turned into a house, barn, corrals, an older mobile home set up on cement blocks. Once again he was going at no more than twenty, this time because his foot felt as numb as the rest of him—numb and sick and filled with dread and something powerful centered in his groin.

He nearly passed the long drive leading away from the road, then punched the brakes. As the car rocked to a stop, he stared out at cows and calves, chickens in the dirt drive, a half dozen fruit trees between the house and mobile home, some cottonwoods, a large, color-strewn flower bed and near that an extensive garden. He contemplated the necessity of a good working well, then surrendered to what screamed inside him.

Obsession. Insanity.

Under him, the car began to vibrate. With an effort, he

eased up on the accelerator and took his foot off the brake. The vehicle inched forward.

Apprehension? The word didn't come close to describing what he felt.

Dust billowed around him, but he couldn't make himself roll up the window because he needed to get as much air as possible into his lungs. Otherwise he'd spin around and go back to where he belonged.

Only he couldn't because the naked and helpless and compelling woman in the photograph haunted him.

A movement to his right caught Mace's attention. He looked at a clothesline filled with sheets and other garments that danced to the wind's whim. This was the twenty-first century. People no longer hung their clothes out to dry, did they? Only, if he wanted his bedding to smell of sage and spring, that's what he'd do.

Someone stood in the middle of the dancing fabric. The person stopped what he or she was doing to watch him. Through eyes incapable of seeing anything except gray, he took note of long, pale hair blowing around a slender neck. The woman was built along lean lines and dressed in snug, faded jeans and a too-big man's shirt. The wind caught the shirt and pressed it around her. She wore no bra. Her breasts were high and well formed, made to fill a man's hands. Her waist was small, her belly flat, hips right for bearing children and calling men to her.

The photograph he'd found in Ronnie's wallet and now kept in his own hadn't done her justice. From this distance, he couldn't tell much about her eyes except that they were large and locked on him.

Sara Parmenter, staring at him.

Chapter Two

ↇ

The stranger reminded Sara of Lobo, her husband's wolf mix. She'd been both afraid of and drawn to the fierce, remote animal. Most of all she'd envied his strength and self-contained nature. If only she could be more like him. When she'd refused to fuck the 150-pound male, Ronnie had let Lobo out of his pen. For nearly a week, Lobo had remained nearby, mesmerizing her with his wary, hungry look. Ronnie had insisted Lobo was waiting his chance to screw her, but Lobo was a creature of habit and stayed, waiting to be fed. Then he'd taken off, and she'd imagined him running free, becoming one with his environment. Unfortunately, a few weeks later an area rancher had called to say he'd shot Lobo for killing a lamb.

Ronnie had slugged her and bellowed it was her fault. If she'd so much as sucked Lobo's cock, the mixed-breed misfit would still be alive.

Tell this man about feeling closer to a predator than you ever did to your husband. Reveal your secrets and see what he does with them.

Shaken by the thought of exposing anything about herself, Sara reverted to her hard-won ability to shut down her most private emotions. She'd deal with reality and take what came one step at a time, careful not to lose self-control.

"What are you doing with my husband's car?" she demanded as the stranger got out of the vehicle.

"I found it."

The hell you did. "Oh," she said instead. He should have remained in the vehicle she hated, should have kept those long, solid legs, tight ass, and in-your-face cock bulge where she couldn't see them. "Where?"

"In an orchard."

The explanation, if that's what it was, threw her back in time to the day she'd learned her estranged husband had been murdered. Then, although she'd already begun the journey toward making her marriage and everything it entailed part of her past, she'd felt freed from a dungeon. Now, after months of freedom, she once again sensed darkness, chains, rope, and leather. No! Never again!

"You want me to believe you stumbled on this thing—" She jabbed a finger at the sleek, black monster that even layers of grime didn't hide. "In an orchard? What was it doing there?"

"I don't know."

You're lying. Not relying on instinct, she ordered herself to learn what she needed to

"You don't know? Why didn't you leave it there? Oh, I know. You decided finder's keepers."

"If I was into auto theft, I wouldn't be here."

He was right.

"How did you know it belonged here?" she asked. *It doesn't belong anywhere. It should have been buried with Ronnie.*

"The registration was in the glove compartment." His arms had been by his side, his fingers clenched, knuckles white. Now he folded his arms over his chest and stared down at her. "I figured you'd want it back."

"So you drove all the way from—where was it anyway?"

He'd been wearing sunglasses. When he removed them, his dark gray eyes sucked her in. Eyes like that could cast a spell over a woman—most women anyway. Hard experience had rendered her immune. "Yuba City, California," he said.

Where Ronnie had died. Her throat went dry. "Oh." *Damn it. Don't go back to the beaten creature you once were.* "Let me get this right. You found the registration so you know the owner was Ronnie Parmenter. And if you live near Yuba City, you know what happened to him. He was murdered." *Murdered. Gone. Out of my life – except for the nightmares.*

The stranger nodded. Despite the fierce sun, he kept his sunglasses off. To her shock, his eyes spoke to her, stroked and caressed when she hadn't believe it possible. "Yes, I know."

"Why did you come all this way? Ronnie couldn't give you a reward, and I don't want it."

"Why not?"

"Because I don't want anything that'd remind me of him." The words gave her courage. "Not that it's your concern, but Ronnie and I were separated. I'd filed for divorce. In fact – " Her laugh held no joy. "If I hadn't been here when it happened, I'd be the prime suspect."

His features had undergone a subtle but undeniable change. He no longer reminded her of Lobo—except in a primal animal way. She'd sensed he'd been absorbing her and Ronnie's relationship. Could relief be responsible for the lessening of the tension in his muscles? Hardly. He couldn't possibly care about the nuances of a failed marriage.

"I'm sorry." She softened her tone. "I guess I should thank you for what you've done." *Even if I don't know why.* "But I'm not the grieving widow. As for the car, you're welcome to it."

"I don't want it."

Like this man, Lobo used to stand motionless while his eyes absorbed everything. Lobo had accepted his body as a powerful tool, something he trusted and which had never failed him. The man's muscles had been honed into steel by whatever he did for a living. His flesh was deeply tanned. He exuded—surely not sexuality. *Then what should you call it?*

"Why not?" she asked. "It doesn't have many miles on it because Ronnie pulled it behind his rig. He was a long-distance trucker. Just take it. Get it out of my sight. Sell it. Pocket the money."

"I don't need the money, Mrs. Parmenter."

Don't call me that. "Fine! Donate it to charity. Just don't let a young driver get his hands on it. It's made for speeding."

He nodded, his first movement in maybe a minute. Then he put back on his sunglasses. Instead of being relieved, she felt denied of something vital and long missing from her life. "What's your name?"

"Mace Seeger." He held out his hand.

Take it. Just take it.

On legs that felt all nerve endings and no muscle, she stepped toward Mace Seeger. Up close, he was taller than she'd hoped. He smelled of sweat and dust and sage. Keeping her expression neutral, she extended her hand, noting that the sun had tanned both of them the same shade. His hand, of course, was larger, but she took pride in the strength in her grip. His fingers closed around hers, matching bone to bone. His fingertips pressed into her flesh and forged a path up her arm, over her breasts, down to her belly. The sensation ended between her legs.

Unnerved and hungry in a way she'd forgotten was possible, she fought to keep her unwanted reaction to herself. Then, almost as if she'd been struck by lightning, fear slammed into her. She jerked free and stumbled back.

"What is it?" he asked and stepped forward.

"No!" She held her hands before her as she'd done too many times in her marriage. "I don't like to be touched."

The instant the words were out, she regretted them. "Look, Mace, seeing that car brings back memories I've spent the past six months putting behind me." She forced her hands into her back pockets. Uncontained by a bra—who needed one when you don't expect to see anyone except Ronnie's parents all day?—her breasts felt too large and sensitive. Her nipples had hardened, and the limp old cotton shirt revealed their condition.

They want your hands, Mace Seeger, their message said. But of course that was ridiculous.

A hot wind raced across the prairie, and although she turned from it, it flattened her shirt against her breasts. The cotton felt like sandpaper. She sucked in the heated air.

"Wait a minute," she heard herself say. "You knew the car's owner had been murdered, right?"

"Right."

"Then why didn't you turn it over to the police?"

"I had my reasons," he said after a moment.

"What does that mean?"

He shook his head. "Nothing. According to the news, the police had no suspects. Having the victim's car in their possession wouldn't accomplish anything. I decided to see if his family had a better use for it."

You're lying. I don't know how I know, but I do. "I-I appreciate the gesture, but I don't want it."

"You resent the money he spent on a toy?"

If only it was that simple? "What do you care?" she demanded. "If you think I'm flattered because you're checking me out," she said, "you're mistaken."

His features shadowed. He ran his hands down his thighs, and her thoughts, her emotions went with the gesture. A lifetime ago she'd been a sexual woman, a willing and eager bed partner. But the realities of her marriage had stripped that from her. Granted, long after she'd stopped responding to him, Ronnie had forced climaxes from her, but even as she screamed her release, she'd hated every sound and movement—the ones he'd allowed her. She'd never go back to letting a man control her body, never!

Still, the fantasies of a young and so-innocent woman remained; either that or the hot-wind day and this man had rekindled them. If she wasn't who she was and if he hadn't driven that damnable car and lied to her, maybe she'd let her body speak to his. In the silent language of sex and trust—a word she barely comprehended — they'd feed off each other. Her fingers ached with the need to touch what she believed she never would again, to close around his cock and caress his genitals. She'd cradle his balls, lift and protect and shelter them while her pussy burned and flooded. The smell of sex would fill the air. They'd look into each other's eyes and say things that didn't need words. Things she must have once believed in.

If she was anyone but who she'd become, his fingers would flow over her hips, press against her belly, and cover her mons. He'd cup her ass and pull her against his hard, hot cock. Joyous, she'd turn her body over to him by opening her legs and inviting him in. He'd come at her in gentleness and urgency, breathing quick and hard, mouth open, hands here, there, everywhere on her lonely flesh.

She might cry; there might be no way she could hide her delight at the end to her long, lonely nights. She wouldn't, couldn't explain her tears.

He wouldn't care. If they fucked — if this frightening and courageous and insane fantasy came true — she'd present her body to him without reservation. He'd respond by burying his cock in her inch by glorious inch. Once they'd found the right rhythm, they'd ride and ride and ride together, learning and giving before climaxing. With his withering cock still in her, they'd share their sweat. Maybe they'd fall asleep in each other's arms.

What was it like to trust a man that much?

"Sara! Sara, where are you?"

Esta Parmenter's question coming from the distant farmhouse yanked Sara back to reality. Oh god, her hands had gone to the inside of her thighs. Although she ordered herself not to look in Mace's eyes, she did.

I know a great deal about you, they said.

Chapter Three

෨

As Sara called out to the older woman, Mace struggled to shake free of whatever the hell had overcome him. Unfortunately, it was going to take his hungry cock longer to get the message.

Sara Parmenter was no longer the helpless and overwhelmed woman he'd seen in the photograph. Instead, Ronnie's widow had turned out to be a long, lean, luscious woman who looked as untamed as her surroundings. She reminded him of an antelope—free and wise, wary, curious, in tune with her body.

Or was she, he pondered as she left him to meet the approaching woman, her hips swaying like prairie grass. Being in tune with one's body meant having control over it, right? If he was a judge of such things, which he sure as hell wasn't, Sara hadn't expected to react to him the way she had. Her hardening nipples and the way she'd ran her hands over her thighs—she was in need of servicing.

Why not? After all, her husband had been dead for half a year, and she was stuck out here miles from civilization.

Maybe she has a lover.

No. A strange man who has just handed her painful memories doesn't turn on a woman who is satisfied in bed. And she *had* been turned on, as had he.

Well, fine. There's two of us then needing to be serviced and serve.

"Are you insane?" he muttered. "Get away. Just get away before she destroys you and what matters to you."

If that's what you want, then why the hell did you come here?

Because her eyes in the picture — haunted, powerful.

Feeling as if he was being pulled against his will, he walked toward Sara and the prairie-faded woman. He saw no physical resemblance between the two, and yet they were comfortable in each other's presence. As he joined them, Sara put her arm around the other woman's shoulder. This time when Sara looked at him, there was nothing sexual in her gaze. Instead, she'd become a wary animal unsure whether to fight or flee.

"That's Ronnie's car," the older woman said. She made no move toward it.

"Yes, it is, Mom." Sara's lips were thin, her body tense. It called to him as nothing ever had. "This man — Mace Seeger — found it and brought it here."

"You — you did?" Tears glistened in the woman's eyes. "He was such a good boy, so full of energy. And when he laughed — did you know? My Ronnie is dead. Someone killed him."

Sara positioned herself so she was between him and the woman she'd called Mom. He had no doubt she'd attack if he tried to harm *Mom.* Someone with this much passion — what had he gotten himself into?

"He knows," Sara said softly. "Mace, this is Ronnie's mother, Esta. She and her husband adopted him when he was a little boy."

"And you're living here with your — your in-laws?" *But you said you'd separated from Ronnie.*

"That's right," she snapped as if reading his mind. She was like quicksilver, her body constantly challenging him. He felt her heat, her energy. Her need.

"Sara has been wonderful," Esta said, wiping away tears. "Living all the way out here with us hasn't been easy for her. Jerome — that's my husband — Jerome and I are so grateful for her help. I don't know how we'd keep this place going without her. We raise cattle and grow a few crops, mostly wheat. The garden is hers, as are the flowers. Come harvest or round-up time, we hire extra help, but usually it's just the three of us." She sighed. "It's a hard life, one we can't do any more."

"Mom, he doesn't care."

"Yeah, I do," Mace said, meaning it. "I'm an orchardist so I know about trying to wrestle a living from the land."

"You are?" Sara and Esta said at the same time. The look Sara gave him, accusing him of keeping something from her, made him glad she couldn't comprehend how many secrets he held.

"That's where I found your son's car," he said. Despite Sara's disapproving glare, he proceeded to tell Esta a lie about how he'd come across the abandoned vehicle. When he found the registration, he recognized the name as the victim of a recent unsolved murder.

"Mom," Sara said. She stared at him with those hungry eyes of hers. "He said he decided to bring it here instead of turning it over to the police. That's what doesn't ring true for me."

"Sara, Sara." Esta patted her hand—the one he'd give anything to have wrapped around his cock. "Mace, she wasn't always like this, suspicious. Despite her hard upbringing, she was a trusting person. But—" Esta sighed. "Things change. Sara, sometimes people do things because they have good hearts."

"Not always."

"Sara! Oh my, where are my manners? You must be tired, hungry, thirsty."

He hadn't eaten or slept since leaving northern California, but what he felt wasn't a hunger food would satisfy. Sara under him—or over him if that's the way things played out— was what he needed.

"Thirsty," he heard himself say. "If you have some water—"

"Right out of the well. Cold and sweet," Esta gushed. She

took his hand. "Come in, please. Let's get you out of the sun."

Mace let Esta lead him toward the old farmhouse with its decaying roof and sagging porch. The stairs creaked under his weight, and he avoided a board because it looked cracked. Winter storms had taken their toil on the unpainted wood siding.

Esta went in ahead of him, and he stepped back so Sara could follow her. Sara stopped at the entryway, blocking it with her body, and half turned toward him. "Don't hurt them," she hissed. "I mean it. Don't say anything to hurt them."

"I don't want to."

"But you might?"

He shrugged and placed his hands in front of her, palms up. For a moment, he thought she was going to take them, and his mind leapt to questions of what she'd do with his hands once they were under her control—maybe place them over her breasts, maybe between her legs. She needed that. Damn, the need cried out in her every nerve ending.

Instead, she placed her own hand around her throat in a self-protective gesture. "If it's going to happen, at least let me know ahead of time," she whispered. "I'll do anything to protect them. Anything."

"Including staying out here instead of living your own life?"

"You don't know anything about me."

But he did, more than she could comprehend.

"Please," she whispered. "Their lives have been hard."

"So has yours."

Her eyes widened. "What—?"

"That's what Esta said."

"Oh," she said on a breath of relief.

She turned from him and stepped into the shadowed interior, then stopped. Against all sanity, he reached out and pressed his palm against her ass. She shuddered. He spread his fingers slightly, and she widened her stance. He slid his fingers between her legs and absorbed her warmth and felt dampness. She shifted her weight and trapped him with her thighs. Calling himself insane, he used his thumb to probe for her cunt. She leaned toward him, sagging really. He heard her quick intake of breath and felt lightheaded.

In reality they probably remained like that no more than a couple of seconds, but the scene cemented itself in his mind and cock. He wasn't just hot and bothered but changed by the primitive connection—changed when that was the last thing he needed.

Over the next half-hour, Mace got to know Esta and her husband Jerome, a scarecrow of a man maybe five foot seven with most of his hair and two fingers on his right hand gone. Everything about Jerome Parmenter said he was heart and soul a rancher, but the harsh seasons had taken their toll. Learning they hadn't given birth to Ronnie helped. Maybe if he didn't know from firsthand experience how hard their lifestyle was, he wouldn't have felt this connection, but he did. He hadn't lost any fingers, and yet his and Jerome's muscles came from the same source, a physical life.

More than that, damn it, they were decent people. He could understand, at least a little, why Sara had remained with them.

At the moment, although Sara had protested, Esta was opening a photograph album. He steeled himself for pictures of Ronnie as a child. Instead, the partly filled album consisted of wedding pictures. At Esta's insistence, Sara had sat next to him. Their bodies weren't touching, not that it lessened his awareness of her. Something flowed out of her to encircle him. He felt whatever it was on and over and around his cock and balls, but it was more than that, a hell of a lot more.

"Doesn't he look handsome?" Esta asked. She sounded a little desperate. "That boy, he hated getting dressed up, but he did for Sara that day."

Teeth clenched, Mace forced himself to focus. Ronnie had a bushy beard, and his hair was long, making it difficult to determine much about his features. The white shirt and tie were conservative, but darkness surrounded the man. The photograph was a full-body shot of the wedding couple so he couldn't tell anything about Ronnie's eyes, yet sensed that was where the darkness centered.

In contrast to the stiff, somber Ronnie, Sara was truly a vision in loveliness. A full head shorter than Ronnie, she stood with her hands demurely in front of her and holding a small bouquet. Ronnie had his arm around her, but it didn't look like they were leaning toward each other. Her eyes were wide, maybe disbelieving, her lips parted in what seemed awe.

Her dress, God, her dress! Feeling as if he'd been touched with a cattle prod, Mace stared at the simple white gown. It flowed over Sara's body, kissed her breasts, waist, and hips before sliding soft-as-rainwater over her legs. He didn't know what the neckline was called, low enough so it showed her collarbone and just a hint of her breasts. There were short, loose sleeves. He couldn't begin to guess at the fabric. To his unpracticed eye, the dress didn't appear to be expensive, and there was no veil or train.

What had hit him like electricity was the sense that he'd seen it in some shape or form before—maybe whispering at the edges of his consciousness. And it wasn't just the dress— the wearer was part of something he already knew.

"There," Esta said, pointing. "There's a close-up of them. Don't they look happy?"

Happy, no. In the shot that showed them from the shoulders up, Sara's expression still held that mix of awe and disbelief. Her smile seemed not really forced, but hardly filled with happiness. Ronnie wasn't smiling. Then, although it took effort, he studied Ronnie Parmenter's dark, almost black eyes. They were set deep in his skull and shielded by thick brows, but that didn't protect him from their impact.

This man was trouble, danger, uneasy in his own body

and at odds with the world. There was also a hint of sorrow and a note of loneliness but what made the greatest impact was something akin to a junkyard dog. Turn your back on him and he'd rip you open.

How…why had Sara married him?

"We were so happy for Ronnie," Esta exclaimed. "Restless the way he was, we weren't sure he'd ever marry, but then Sara came along, and it was love at first sight—for both of them."

No it wasn't.

With a shock, Mace realized the thought hadn't been his but Sara's. He looked at her.

They don't understand, her eyes said. *And neither do you.*

Chapter Four

🔊

Sara walked ahead of Mace to the barn. Every ounce of self-preservation in her screamed to find a way to make him leave, but here she was fulfilling Esta's request to set their guest up in the sleeping room that had been incorporated into the barn.

Esta had bustled about the kitchen preparing dinner and showing more energy and enthusiasm than she had since they'd received word of Ronnie's murder. Mace and Jerome had talked at length about whether it was worth trying to repair the old tractor. After dinner, they'd gone out to look at the machinery while she and Esta cleaned up. Then they'd all sat around talking about the price of hay and falling water tables and government regulations.

She'd been far enough away from Mace so she shouldn't have felt his—his whatever it was he sent out. Unfortunately, she couldn't stop studying his economical movements, the way his expressive hands punctuated his words. She'd tried and failed to keep her eyes on his face. When her attention strayed elsewhere, it invariably settled on his crotch.

This man had put his hand against her crotch earlier. Instead of yelling he had no right, she'd ached to suck him into her. If they'd stayed like that much longer, she would have launched herself at him.

Her eyes burned, and it was all she could do to blink back tears. *Don't think about what Ronnie stole from you, don't!*

Once inside the barn, she reached for the light switch. The main area was immediately bathed in light, but shadows clung to the edges. At the moment, there were two pregnant mares in the stalls, and she went to check on them. Although both

31

mares' bags leaked milk, neither was in labor.

"They weren't planned pregnancies," she told Mace so she'd have something to say. "A neighbor's stallion got loose and by the time we found him on our acreage, it was too late. With Jerome and Esta hoping to sell, we're trying to keep the livestock to a minimum—just run enough cattle to keep the operation going."

"Sell? They're sure?"

Mace stood behind her. She turned, both relieved to find him several feet away and too aware of how natural he looked standing on scattered straw with a coiled rope near his arm. All he lacked were cowboy boots and a hat.

"Yes." Her mouth went dry. "They've been talking about it ever since they realized Ronnie wasn't going to help them run it. Then when he was killed…"

"How did you learn?"

"What?"

He took a couple of steps closer. Behind her, one of the mares sighed. "The three of you were here, right? How did you find out he'd been—murdered?"

Was Mace becoming larger, or was it her imagination? God but he was beautiful, all male with powerful thighs and lean hips, no stomach. His shoulders—why did they have to be so broad as if capable of carrying the world's weight—or her to a bed?

"I, ah, a sheriff's deputy drove out and told us."

"How did you feel, Sara? When you learned you'd never see your husband again, how did you feel?"

His words challenged her as surely as a cougar challenged the lives of newborn calves. But could the onslaught of emotions come from another source—one tied in with her nightmares?

"Free," she said and took her own step toward him.

"Why?"

"We were separated."

"If you were divorcing him, why would you want him dead?"

She felt splintered, muscles losing connection with her bones, nerves reaching beyond the barrier her skin provided. "You didn't know Ronnie Parmenter so you can't possibly understand what he was like."

Yes, I did.

Startled by her comprehension of his silent response, she struggled to regain her equilibrium. "He, ah, he didn't want the separation. He refused to sign divorce papers. It was going to be a long, drawn out process."

"But you didn't want to stay married to him?"

"No!"

"Then why did you marry him, Sara?"

She couldn't continue to face him, not with his hard question between them and feeling his body snaking around hers—at least in her mind. She tried to back away but bumped into a railing. Unsure of her plans, she stepped into the open area they called the arena. Now she felt vulnerable and exposed.

"Don't, please," Mace said and touched her. It was a little thing, his fingers light on her upper arm.

She felt herself lean into the contact. The tears she'd struggled against returned.

"I don't want to hurt you, Sara," he whispered. "You've already been hurt enough."

He didn't know about her life, did he? His hand slid like rain down her arm to take her hand. He drew her closer and settled his other hand over her hip.

"I saw your wedding picture," he continued. "You weren't the blushing bride. Neither was Ronnie the besotted groom."

"No."

"Then what brought you together?"

She tried to pull free; she really did. But he'd struck a fire between her legs—no, not just there, in her pussy, her cunt, her too-long dormant clit.

"I was alone," was the only thing she could think to say. "So was he."

"You're a beautiful woman, Sara. Any number of men—"

She laughed, the sound resigned. "Look around. How many other people do you see? The nearest town is nearly fifty miles away."

"Then why didn't you move years ago?"

I didn't know where I belonged; I'm not sure I ever have. "A lot of reasons none of which I have to go into with you." Although she'd placed her hand on his hip for balance—surely for no other reason—she told herself he didn't know that her clit-fire continued to rage.

He didn't speak which left her with the terrible responsibility of filling the silence. She supposed she could tell him any number of things, such as her plan to go to college once she and her in-laws were free of the ranch, but her hopes and dreams weren't his business.

"You still haven't adequately explained why you're here," she said although she doubted she'd get more of an answer than she already had. "If—do you know something about Ronnie's death you haven't told us?"

Suddenly his hands were on her ass, fingers spread over her buttocks. He forced her close. Her arms went around his neck, and they stood cock to belly, leaning back slightly. One of the mares neighed, the other nickered in reply.

He stood too close for her to see his features clearly, but it was safer this way. Or was it? Without the distraction of trying to read his eyes, she had little to do except absorb his sexuality. The message in his hard, thrusting cock needed no explanation. She'd turned him on—she who had spent so much of her married life feeling like a sexual object and not a human being.

The heat-hunger she'd fought since Mace Seeger had stepped out of the car kicked up more notches than she could count. She should have fought it. But it felt so good!

Her mind opened, expanded, and sought new horizons. He'd folded himself over her, and yet having him everywhere didn't intimidate her. Instead, she gave into a wonderful and wild fantasy.

In her newly free mind, their clothes were no more, and he'd knelt before her. His mouth settled on her mons, his tongue making hot forays past her pubic hair to unbelievably sensitive flesh. She *felt* his thumb work between her ass cheeks, press against her anus, and slide forward. Just as he reached her starving and heated labia, he reversed direction. His thumb became a feather barely tracking what he'd already claimed. She longed to trap him by squeezing her buttocks together, but the way his tongue brushed her made that impossible.

Was it physically possible for a man to work both tongue and thumb like this? But if she separated any part of herself from the incredible sensation long enough to ask, she might miss something important.

Important? Try vital, lifesaving, reborn!

His tongue no longer bathed her mons but had journeyed to her labia. Maybe he wanted to make up for what his thumb hadn't accomplished. His thumb? Where—oh, yes, nearly to the small of her back now. Only it wasn't just his thumb any more. His fingers danced lightly at the edge of her crack. Sometimes they pushed as if trying to bore a hole through to her pussy. Sometimes they radiated out to ignite everything from the waist down.

Too late she realized he'd taken her clit in his mouth. She had no fight in her, not a single thought not connected with her need for climax. With his tongue and teeth and lips showing her the way, she surged upward.

A mare whinnied, the sound sharp. Mace's grip shifted to her upper arms, holding her in place while he studied the animal. "Is this her first?" he asked.

She didn't want to talk about laboring horses, or anything else. The approaching fantasy-fueled ecstasy had already tamped down, and she needed it back.

"I shouldn't—" His hold on her arms tightened. "We shouldn't—damn you." He pulled her against him, his chest flattening her breasts. She felt as if she'd been thrown into the ocean with a wave fast approaching. She looked up. His mouth, hard and insistent claimed hers and sealed her will to his. In her mind, the wave and his mouth became one.

Surrender, let him take over and run you out to sea.

It felt wonderful with the current all around and her small and willing in its grip. This ocean felt warm almost to the point of hot. She vaguely realized he now massaged where he'd gripped earlier, and they'd both opened their mouths. His tongue tasted hers. Then it was her turn, and she ventured in, lathed her tip over the inside of his cheeks. She couldn't put a name to the taste, a mix of what he'd had for dinner including the beer Jerome had given him along with something that was uniquely, privately him.

She took that privacy, that uniqueness and pulled it into herself. The moment she did, it forged a molten path down her throat. Her legs separated of their own will to allow him closer. He stepped into what she'd offered and after wrapping his arms around her middle, he bent her back until she would have fallen if it hadn't been for him.

His height and bulk wasn't made for folding over a woman. But they did this thing together, her spine arching back, his bending forward. Their mouths continued as one. She tasted him, smelled him, felt him. She couldn't feel her clothing or surroundings, didn't remember her name.

He was everywhere again, a damnable ocean wave and she a small animal riding each swell and dip. Her cunt turned liquid and loose and wet from her sex juices. His cock drove into her belly. She didn't know enough about its size and texture, its strengths and weaknesses, how much cum it held and what that cum felt like filling her. But she could imagine.

Could learn and be taught.

Her imagination filled her. She now saw herself on her belly, ass lifted by the pillows under her pelvis. Her head lay to the side, cheek flat against the sheet. She had no place to put her arms; maybe they didn't exist.

He'd bent her knees and spread her legs, positioning her so she was fully accessible to him.

His tongue came at her, bathing her labial lips. They felt swollen, flooded by the cunt juices that flowed endlessly. She heard him drink of her offering, felt him use his tongue to pull more and more fluid into his mouth.

He must have drunk his fill because he'd turned his attention to her labial lips. He closed his lips around one, cradled it, then tugged gently. She tried to shift her weight so she could follow him, but the position he'd placed her in left her with no freedom.

No freedom.

She sealed her mind away from the thought, tried to anyway, and went back to experiencing, growing, becoming a woman.

On lonely nights when it had been just her and the stars, she'd sat on the porch playing music on her CD. Her taste ran from country and western to ethnic instrumentals, anything that felt in tune with her surroundings and moods. During hot, endless summer nights and even winter when the wind threatened to rip her coat from her body, she went beyond thought to emotion, to feeling things she had no words for, sensations at one with the tears she didn't dare shed. If she was certain Esta and Jerome wouldn't come outside, she'd unzip her jeans and play with herself until she could no longer control her breathing.

Then she'd take her hot and bothered body and CD

player into the room where Mace would spend tonight, tear off her clothes, collapse on the bed and spread her legs. Often she had to bite her tongue to keep from crying out at the moment of self-driven climax. In winter she'd have to crank up the portable heater; in summer the air would feel close and heavy.

Not thinking, she'd cup a hand over a breast and tease her nipple to hardness while sticking her fingers far inside her vagina. Sometimes they grew tired before she made it over the edge, but because she didn't have a choice—not if she was going to function during the day—she probed and teased until she found the path to release.

When she was on the same wavelength with her sex, the climax came quick and hard enough to leave her shaken. Other times only lightly playing with her clit brought release.

Manipulating her clit, wonderful as it felt, always left her uneasy. With her fingers inside her, she could chart her progress. Her clit, however, like her heart, resisted control. It was always responsive—and that was the problem.

Her musing about masturbation, although multi-layered, came all at once, one thought beginning before another had ended. In the process, she lost hold of what was going on between her and Mace.

Frightened, she tried to assess. She was still off-balance, but they were no longer tongue fucking. He'd maneuvered her hands behind her and held her wrists. Her legs were inside his, and his calves pressed against hers, his thighs sealing her in place.

She tried to pull her hands free, but he wouldn't let her. She pulled again, just testing of course, not yet desperate. He kept her hands tight against her backside.

For a moment—maybe less than that—it was all right. She'd been alone for so long, maybe her entire life. It was time—she wanted it, didn't she—to give herself body and soul to a man and become that man's woman. To trust.

Then memories of other helplessness slammed into her,

and fear sucked her in.

"No!" she screamed. She twisted to one side and then the other. Sweat broke out between her breasts. "No!"

Mace released her and pulled her into an upright position. Then he stepped back, his arms by his side, hands fisted.

"Sara, what is it?"

"I don't like—" She backed away and held her hands in front of her, palms up to protect her face and throat as she'd done too many times. "I don't like to be touched."

Chapter Five

ℬ

The sheet smelled of Sara.

It might not be the sheet, Mace admitted as he struggled to find a comfortable position on the single bed. After what had taken place before she'd turned tail and fled, no wonder he hadn't yet exorcised her from his system.

Exorcised? Yeah, maybe it would take a priest's incantations to rid himself of her impact.

Why? What was this connection between them? Did it go deeper than his role in Ronnie's death or — his hand stole to his cock, distracting him from the unwanted question. The most unnerving thing in a constantly growing list of unnerving things was his lack of self-control around her. Because his work was ruled by the seasons, he was accustomed to having things in the hands of the fates. As a result, his personal existence had become one of simplicity. When time allowed, he climbed onto his dirt bike and traveled down long, lonely roads far from freeways and cities. He packed a bedroll and simple foods, a fishing pole and whatever he was reading. He'd return with the beginning of a beard, dust in his hair, sunburned and at peace.

As for women, he'd had as many as time and circumstances allowed. Because few available women hung out in almond orchards, he went in search — anything from bars to county fairs. He never had trouble finding a sex partner. He was reasonably attractive in a weathered way, and the women said they loved his strong, hard body. Mostly they raved about his performance in the sack.

All well and good, what man didn't like being considered a stud? But those relationships, although some had lasted for months, had ended. He'd always been the one to leave and like it or not had become expert in shaking off those who resisted ending things.

As for why he stopped calling someone like Angie with her flaring hips and D cups or Heather who had her own dirt bike and embraced long camping trips or Deb, a woman of mind-blowing intelligence and climaxes—the hell of it was, he didn't know.

Sara's just another conquest, he told himself with his fingers expertly cupped around his aching cock and his wrist and forearm engaged in short, hard pumps.

He lay naked on his back, legs splayed for better access, and stared at the ceiling. He tried to think of something, anything other than where he was and why, but his mind refused to obey. Instead, as his manipulation picked up speed, he imagined what Sara was doing and thinking.

Was she, like him, engaged in self-release?

Maybe she was devising a way to get rid of him.

Do it, for both our sakes.

And if she didn't, if instead she walked into this room all naked and ready, eyes smoky, her body reaching for his?

She'd look down at him with a half smile on the beautiful lips that didn't smile enough. *"I can do better,"* she'd tell him, indicating his nearly frenzied masturbation. *"Let me show you."*

Not waiting for his reply, she'd climb onto the bed and straddle him, her knees against his hips, her breasts reaching for him as she bent over to kiss his throat and chest. Somehow, although she was so damn ripe, so incredibly beautiful, he'd force himself to remain still.

She was a long, lean woman who ate only to fuel muscle and bone. Her breasts were large in contrast with the rest of her, not oversized but full and rich, ripe for a man's hands and mouth. In his mind, she teased him with those breasts. Leaning closer and arching her back at the same time, she let the hard nipples graze his chest. Over and over she gave him a taste of herself, but when he tried to seal her to him, she shook her head and pulled away.

You're mine this time, she'd say. *When you stormed into my life, I didn't know what to do with you, but now I do.*

Shit, did she! Her body became snakelike, gliding effortlessly over him, touching places he barely knew he had, leaving her impact everywhere. Her laughter became fuller, richer; he took her joy into him, and it became part of him.

She scooted further down on the bed so her pussy was over his cock. Still she kept space between them and teased him in a way that made him want to bellow. Delicious anticipation curled around him, and he relished where he was in sexual need.

His body caught fire, his every nerve crackling and hot. He barely existed beyond his cock and no longer had control over his most precious organ. It had become her plaything, her slave.

And what a willing slave it was. In the mysterious workings of his imagination, she'd repositioned herself so her open mouth was just over his cock. Desperate to obey, he lifted himself as best he could off the bed and offered himself up to her.

She came at him slow. Bit by incredible bit the feel of her moist breath on his tip became warmer. Then, when he was certain he'd die from the wanting, she touched him with the tip of her damp tongue. Pre-cum sprang free. Chuckling low, she drank his offering. Next she ran her tongue down one side of his cock and then the other. His fingers gripped the sheet so tightly he thought he'd tear the fabric or his nails, maybe both. Needing to touch her, but not daring to, made his head roar. His ass muscles clenched and remained that way.

Done with her cock bathing, she turned her attention to the base and took his balls in her hand. She sheltered them in her palm, jiggled and pinched lightly.

He couldn't keep track of the bombarding sensations.

Every fiber in him screamed to grab hold of her hips and force her cunt over and around his cock, but the hell of it was, he was afraid. She controlled the flow of their fuck.

It was impossible; he knew it was. But he was absolutely, completely convinced she'd found a way to place her other hand on his throat. Now he had three things to keep track of — her tongue caressing his cock, one hand doing things to his balls that kept him uneasy and unbalanced and delighted, and now long, strong fingers pressing against the base of his throat. If she cut off his air, he'd shove her away, fight her, overpower her. Maybe.

And maybe he'd let her kill him and be done with it.

Ready? she asked.

Ready, he told her.

Finally, thankfully, she opened her pussy for him. He wanted to go at it slow and draw out his reward, but his cock was having none of that. Wild, he plunged into her, ramming deep. She felt wet, hot and drenched, smelling of sex.

Like a cowgirl on a stud, she rode him. Like a stallion at the start of a race, he gave her muscle and nerve and bone. Most of all he gave her his cum, his climax. He heard her scream but knew precious little else.

* * * * *

It was barely light when Mace walked into the ranch house. Jerome had told him they never locked their door and for him to come in as soon as he got up. Esta had showed him where the coffeepot was. All he had to do was turn it on.

After the night he'd had, he needed a lot of coffee. The single beer he'd drunk before dinner shouldn't have given him a hangover, but he had one. He wasn't yet awake enough to remember much except the most productive masturbation he'd ever had.

The door squeaked when he opened it, and he made a mental note to look at the hinges. The place needed so much work. The most pressing need was a new roof, and although Jerome had bought the necessary material, he hadn't begun. If he stayed, Mace thought as he stood in the silent living room, he'd do that.

By switching his attention from his growing to-do list to what the house was telling him, he detected snoring sounds from Jerome and Esta's room. He stepped closer. They were both loudly asleep, old people in unison. Sara no longer lived in the mobile home but slept in what had been Esta's sewing room. Sara's features had remained carefully neutral when she explained that it made no sense to keep two sets of utilities going.

Instead of turning on the coffee he badly needed, he walked over to the small room. The door wasn't completely closed, and although he couldn't see inside, he swore he felt her presence. Well, why the hell not? After all, she'd fucked him last night—or at least her ghost had.

Although he risked being thrown out on his ears, he pushed on the door. This one didn't squeak. When he heard her deep, regular breathing, he slipped in.

There weren't any curtains on the window, and the new morning provided just enough light so he could make out her bed. She hadn't done much to turn the room into a bedroom, but he didn't dwell on it. How could he when she lay curled on her side, naked except for the sheet and single blanket that came to her waist? No wonder she'd tucked her hands between her legs; she was trying to stay warm.

Or was she? Maybe, like him, she'd fallen asleep with her thoughts and fingers on her sex organs.

Grateful for the rag rug under his shoes, he inched closer. Her hair had fallen across her cheek, and his observation of her form was more imagination than reality.

If he sat on the side of the bed and touched her, would she reach for him? Could she somehow be aware of her role in his self-gratification and want to participate in the reality? In his imagination, the answer was an unqualified *yes*.

She moaned and flung out an arm. He waited for her to relax. Instead, she moaned again, the sound sharper.

Although he wanted to help her past what might be an unsettling dream, he simply watched because he didn't want to risk frightening her. With jerky and uncertain movements, she turned onto her back and gave him a thought-stealing view of her breasts. Her eyes remained closed. She tucked her legs close to her ass, and her hands were in front of her, palms up in the self-protective position she'd assumed last night.

She began to cry, not the kind of sobs that might lead to a cleansing of the spirit, but small and helpless.

Can't breathe. Can't run – nowhere to hide. He's dark, dark and deadly. He's so big; he's become the world. He's coming for me. I'm trapped. He's going to kill me this time. I know he is.

What have I done? Why do you hate me so much?

Closer, smelling of decay, big as the world and even stronger, smiling a smile with no warmth in it. Eyes dead – no, not dead but without hope or humanity.

He's raising his hand, stalking closer. His body says he knows he has me and I have nowhere to go, no one to turn to.

A weapon! I need a weapon. But my hands are empty. Will he find my throat? Is that what he wants, to rip open my veins so he can watch me bleed to death? How long will it take; what will he do to me while I'm dying?

Oh God, another step! Now his features are no longer cloaked in night. I can see, can see –

Ronnie.

Oh Ronnie, I thought I knew you.

A shake of the head as if he'd read her mind, and he took another deadly, taunting step. She heard herself whimper and hated the sound. If she was going to die, she'd inflict as much damage to her killer/husband as possible.

"Hands over your head," he demanded. "You know the drill. *Down on your knees, forehead touching the ground, hands still*

45

high."

"No! No more!"

"Bitch! You know what happens when you try to defy me."

She did. Oh god, she did!

Biting her tongue to keep from begging for the mercy that never came, she gathered her muscles and watched him in the way of a trapped animal.

"You're mine," he said. "No other man touches you, understand!"

"But you're dead."

His laugh coated the air in black. "How can that be, bitch? I'm here, aren't I?"

"I-I don't understand."

"I'll never die, Sara. You'll never be free of me. Never."

"Why? What do you want with me?"

"Your body. Your soul."

"No!"

"Yes. On your knees, bitch. Head down. Open your ass to me, again and again!"

"No!" Sara screamed and sat up.

She'd just begun to comprehend that she was in the sewing room when she became aware of another presence. The helpless whimper Ronnie had loved wrenching from her clogged her throat. Although she hated herself for it, she covered her throat.

"Go away," she hissed. "Go away."

"I can't, Sara."

Not Ronnie's voice. "Who—?" she started to say. Then she felt a different, less deadly male presence. "Mace? What are you doing in here?"

He stood only a couple of feet away. "I heard you," he said. "You were having a nightmare."

What goes beyond a nightmare? What name goes with being

treated like a piece of meat? "I don't want you here! You have no right—"

"The hell I don't, Sara." He glanced at his arms, then folded them over his chest. "We've gone way beyond being strangers." His mouth tightened as if he was trying to take back his words. "I was concerned for you. Don't try to turn it into a crime."

Concerned for you. How she wanted to believe. She was still trying to deal with her admission when his gaze shifted from her face to her breasts. They heated as she belatedly realized she was naked—something she'd only recently felt comfortable doing.

"This isn't an invitation," she said as she yanked the sheet over her breasts. Her shaking hands made a lie of her speech.

"What was the nightmare about?" he asked and sat on the edge of the bed. His weight on the sheet pulled it down so it now barely covered her nipples. She tugged, but he paid no attention. "Do you have many?"

I used to live a nightmare. "No," she lied.

"What was it about?"

"I-I can't remember."

He shook his head. "Can't or aren't willing to tell me?"

"Whatever. Leave. I want to get dressed."

"Go ahead. I'm not stopping you."

"The hell you aren't!" Strange, arguing with Mace was helping to put the nightmare behind her.

He shifted position and stared at the floor. His hands were on his knees, his breathing an uneasy whisper. He hadn't shaven for several days, but that wasn't what had turned his features dark. She tried not to lose herself in his tousled hair, the bulge nestled between his legs. He pressed his fingers against his forehead, leaving white marks. "I should leave, Sara. For both of us, it's what I should do. But..."

"But what?" The thought of never seeing him again felt

like a vise closing in around her heart.

"The place is going to need work before it'll sell."

"It isn't your responsibility."

"Yeah." He drew out the word. "It is."

"Why?"

She wasn't surprised when he didn't answer. She'd felt so damn vulnerable during her dream—if that's what it had been—and now the same emotion radiated from him.

He stood up, but although she could have reclaimed the sheet, she didn't bother. In the wake of what had happened between them last night, what did naked breasts matter?

"You keep secrets, Sara," he muttered with his back to her. "So do I."

The wrenching pain in his voice brought her to her feet. She'd nearly reached him when she felt something cold grip her throat.

Ronnie!

Chapter Six

ഇ

Why did you say that to her? Mace berated himself as he watched Sara tug on a pair of jeans and a faded shirt that was a twin of the one she'd worn yesterday. He should have known better than to hint at the deeper reason for his coming here. Now he had, she was reacting badly. Not only did her hands shake so she could barely button the shirt—she again hadn't bothered with a bra—but a little while ago she'd stroked her throat as if it had been injured.

Watching her dress had given him a half erection. The pull in his groin had also served as all the warning he needed not to touch her. Maybe, someday, she'd tell him about her nightmare, but she'd expect something from him in return, and he couldn't imagine ever giving her that.

The only bathroom was next to Jerome and Esta's bedroom so he'd waited in the living room when she went in there. She'd only been gone a short while when she returned, her face white.

"What is it?" he demanded.

"No-nothing." She massaged her throat. "I need to check on the brood mares." Her voice rasped, and she winced when she spoke.

Before he could ask if she was all right, she brushed past him and hurried outside. He heard bedsprings creak but didn't wait to see if Jerome and Esta were getting up, Instead he followed the woman who'd changed his life the moment he'd seen the demeaning and erotic photograph.

By the time he'd closed the door, she was already halfway to the barn, her long legs taking her away from him. He was searching for the strength to let her go when he swore he saw a shadow behind her. Alarmed, he hurried after her and into the dimly lit barn.

She turned on him. "I don't need your help. It's not like I haven't helped a mare give—"

A sharp whinny interrupted her. As one, they turned toward the box stall where the sound had come from. Despite the distraction of the heat on his arm because it had briefly brushed her, he had a long way to go before he could shake off the image of that dark shape near her. *Ronnie*, the voice in his head insisted. *Ronnie, come to claim her.*

"The hell he is," he muttered low so Sara couldn't hear. She'd already opened the gate and was kneeling beside the prone and straining mare.

Acknowledging she knew more about the birthing process than he did, he entered the stall but remained against the fencing. He figured Sara would tell him what to do if she needed help. In the meantime, he listened to her calm voice and watched the soothing way she patted the laboring mare's head. The connection between woman and horse seemed complete, two coworkers with the same goal in mind.

The birth took place no more than five minutes later and accomplished with an amazing lack of blood and sweat—at least from his perspective. The mare obviously had done this before and went about pushing out the foal in a businesslike way. As for Sara, she positioned herself at the mare's ass and held the tail out of the way. When the front legs appeared, she gently but firmly pulled the baby out.

"A colt," she announced as the newborn lay scrunched against her thighs. She deftly cleared mucus from the baby's mouth and nose and watched it breathe before scrambling away. Still kneeling on the straw flooring, she softly congratulated the mare who'd gotten to her feet and was licking her infant. The colt kicked his legs a few times, then struggled to a sitting position. He tried to stand but only succeeded in straightening his forelegs. He sat on his rump and looked around at the strange new world he'd found himself in.

"Aren't you going to help him stand?" Mace asked.

"Nope. That's his job. Don't worry. Mom won't let him be lazy."

Sara was right. Soon after being born, the colt was standing on spindly, uncertain legs and nursing, the act accompanied by excited snorts and grunts. Unperturbed, the mare continued nuzzling her son.

Sara joined him at the railing. "I love this," she whispered. Her voice no longer sounded as if her throat hurt. "I don't think I'll ever get over what a miracle birth is."

Although they were so close in the cramped quarters he could barely keep her features clear, he had no trouble making out the sheen of tears. No darkness hovered nearby. Surely he'd only imagined Ronnie's presence.

No. He'd be a fool to believe that.

"It is a miracle," he agreed. "Next to this, watching a tree produce isn't on the same radarscope."

"I'm going to miss this when I leave," she admitted. "But I have to get away."

"You deserve your own life." *In my bed — if we were two different people.*

"It's not just that." After a glance at mother and son, she walked out of the stall. He followed and closed the gate behind him. Before she could put any more space between them, he wrapped his arm around her waist and drew her against him. Because he didn't trust her to stay where he needed her, he pressed his fist against the small of her back before running his free hand down the V of her blouse until he'd covered her breast.

"Don't you own a bra?" He sounded as if his throat had been sandpapered. "I'm not complaining. Believe me, complaining is the last thing I'd do, but you're making me crazy."

"I, ah…"

He wanted her to lean against him and press herself into his hard cock. Hell, his ego needed to be told — with or without words — that he was such a stud she didn't stand a chance against the testosterone oozing from his pores.

"Esta and Jerome," she whispered. "They're going — I know they'll come in to check."

They aren't here yet. Although the soft cotton hampered his movements, he managed to bracket her nipple with his fingers. "Is that what you're trying?" he asked. He hadn't had sex in too damn long; his need was too damn strong. "To drive me crazy by running around braless?"

"N-no."

So much for getting her to melt against him. Except for the soft woman's breast under his control, she felt like coiled wire. Why hadn't she broken free?

"No?" He drew out on the nipple, and it hardened even more. "Why, Sara? Why so few clothes?"

"I'm…trying."

"Trying what?"

"To find myself. To become a woman again."

"What? I don't—"

"Sara? Are you in there?" Esta called out.

Silent as a night animal, Sara slipped out of his grasp. Then she whirled on him, and her eyes, wide and wild, bore into him.

"What?" he demanded.

"He took so much from me," she whispered.

* * * * *

A little more than an hour later, Sara found herself walking toward Mace who stood at the barn's entrance, a tool belt around his narrow waist. In the meantime, Esta and

Jerome had examined the colt and declared it fit; breakfast had been prepared and consumed; she'd taken a shower.

She'd tried to talk herself into staying inside with Esta, but her flesh fairly itched with the need to be near Mace. And, although she hated admitting it, she felt safer near him than away. When she was alone, she sensed *the* presence.

"So..." She tried to smile. "It looks as if Jerome has already put you to work. Where is he?"

Mace pointed toward where their nearest neighbor lived. "He said something about Lou's extension ladder and took off in the truck."

"Then you're going to start work on the roof?"

He patted his belt. "As soon as I build some scaffolding. Jerome said you know where the extra lumber is."

She'd already nodded in that direction when too late she realized the stack of lumber was next to *the trailer*. Any hope she carried that Mace hadn't noticed her reaction faded when he captured her arms and spun her toward him. She strained against his grip but didn't panic.

"What is it?" he demanded.

"The trailer...it's where Ronnie and I lived."

"And the memories aren't good, right?"

Her laugh held no mirth. "Try hell."

He pulled her closer so now she felt nothing except his heat, his maleness. "If you hate it, why haven't you gotten rid of it?" he asked.

She flattened her forearms against his chest, felt her cunt soften and grow wet—turned on by a man when she'd stopped believing herself capable of the emotion. Disbelieving, she longed to stroke Mace's neck and cheeks, but she felt so vulnerable around him—vulnerable and alive.

"Who would want it?" she asked, desperate to stay in the here and now. "It's worthless."

"Then you should have taken it to the dump."

"The only thing that passes for a dump is nearly a hundred miles away. Besides, how would I get it there?" *Can you tell how desperate I am to be fucked? Just fucked. Nothing else.*

"How did it get here?"

"What does it matter? All right! Ronnie's folks had it hauled in when he was a teenager. He didn't want to live under the same roof with the old farts as he called them. And—although they'd never admit it, I don't think they wanted him either."

"What's in it?"

No! I won't go! I can't! "What does it matter?" What if the powers of sex and fear were closely related? Was it possible to want and dread at the same time? "Let it go. Please, let it go!"

"I can't," he said as she knew he would.

*   *   *   *   *

The at least thirty-year-old sun-bleached singlewide trailer smelled like death. With Mace beside her, Sara told herself it wasn't a death-stench but simply the result of stale air and decay. Still, the brittle structure brought back too many memories. Those memories kept her at Mace's side and roped her arm around his waist. He'd draped his arm over her shoulder as they stepped inside, but now his grip was almost painful. Because she'd left the curtains—cheap and faded things she'd sewn and Ronnie had ridiculed—closed, she could barely see.

But she remembered. God, did she!

"You lived in here?" Mace asked.

"Yes."

"How could you stand it?"

He didn't leave me a choice.

"The furniture wouldn't make yard sale rejects and that kitchen, there isn't enough counter space for a toaster."

"I know." She forced herself to step away from Mace. She

didn't want him in here. Damn it, she didn't want him to be part of her past.

"Tell me about it."

Tell you about it. They weren't alone; she knew with every fiber in her that Ronnie had joined them. He'd hear everything they said, see everything.

Fuck you Ronnie! Fuck you and everything you stand for! Die, damn it, die and stay dead!

"He knew I hated it," she said because Mace's eyes gave her courage. "That's why he refused to find another place for us to live."

"Bastard."

The trailer hadn't had any insulation, but Ronnie had fastened sound deadening boards to the walls and ceiling. That way, no matter what happened in here, his parents couldn't hear.

"I didn't know any better, not at first," she admitted. She hugged her middle and pressed her shoes into the filthy carpet and didn't take her eyes off Mace who represented the only spot of life. "The way I grew up—never having anything—I accepted what Ronnie provided. At least at first."

"And then?" Mace clenched his fists. If his shoulders hadn't been so wide and his legs so strong, the trailer would have closed down around him.

I can't do this. I can't. "Then the other things started. Even when…even when I was too scared to think, I vowed I'd get free. Somehow."

"Bastard! Damn fucking bastard."

She couldn't say how she'd gotten into Mace's arms. Maybe they'd both worked at erasing the distance. She pressed her cheek against his shoulder, and her arms clenched his waist so tightly her muscles burned. He held her with equal strength.

"I need it all, Sara."

Tell him and I'll kill you.

Ronnie. "He's in here," she whispered. "I feel him."

"He's dead. He can't hurt you."

I'll kill him too.

"You don't understand." Ronnie was somewhere; she just didn't know where. She'd felt his anger and hatred, but it had never been like this. Before, she'd believed he'd directed his fury at the world and himself. Now, maybe, he didn't know what to do with his rage and so it kept building. But why, after a half-year of being dead, was he making his presence known?

Because he's here. You belong to me, bitch. Always did. Always will.

No, I don't! she raged at her murdered husband.

Mace shook her. "Sara, what is it?"

"M-memories. I'm sorry." She clung to him as she'd never clung to a man.

"You have to get rid of them," he said and began stroking her back. "Starting here. Show me everything."

The insane request made her laugh. "It won't take a minute. Other than the bedroom and bath, this is all there is."

"The two of you were always together?"

"Except when he was on the road. He was gone a lot — looking for horizons."

"And when he returned, you were waiting for him?"

His strokes had reached beyond her skin to bone and muscles. She felt hot and needy. "I don't want to talk about it." *I can't.*

"I understand, but we're going to." He ran his fingers through her hair, not to punish as Ronnie sometimes had. "You know it's the right thing to do. What you need."

What I need is for you to have sex with me until I can't remember Ronnie ever touching me. "I left him," she whispered. "Several times. But I had little money and couldn't get far. He always found me. Brought me back."

"Why didn't his parents stop him?"

"Be-because I didn't tell them."

"Why not?"

"Ronnie said he'd kill me if I did. And them if they tried to protect me."

She waited for another of Mace's hard questions, but he only drew in a long breath and ran his hands over her buttocks. She felt herself seeping into him. The air smelled cleaner. A little more light entered the room.

"Are you all right?" Mace whispered.

"I, ah…"

"Sara, I want to see the bedroom."

After filing a restraining order against Ronnie and starting divorce proceedings, she'd packed her things, locked the door to the trailer, and gone to Prineville where she'd rented an apartment. She hadn't told Jerome and Esta why, and they hadn't asked. Instead, the three of them had waited for Ronnie to return. Because she'd called him on his cell phone to tell him what she'd done, she'd been dreading what would happen.

Instead of a confrontation, however, she'd found herself a widow. There was no reason for not going into the trailer for the few belongings it held, but she hadn't once entered it. Not until today.

Holding Mace's hand, she walked down the short, narrow hall to the bedroom. The door caught as it always had, and she put her shoulder into it. If anything, the room smelled worse than the rest of the place. There was barely enough room for the dresser she and Ronnie had shared, the chair where he'd thrown his clothes and sometimes her, and the bed. She stared at it, remembering the way the springs squeaked, the sagging mattress, the nights.

Taking her with him, Mace walked over to the closet. She thought about telling him he had no right opening it but didn't. That door stuck, too.

"Not much of a handyman was he?" Mace muttered. He poked his head in. "There's not enough room for one person's things let alone two."

"I didn't have much. Neither did Ronnie."

"Hmm." He pulled something off a hanger and held it up. At the sight of her homemade wedding dress, she took an involuntary step back. Then because she couldn't keep him from seeing, she gripped her elbows and waited.

The bodice had been ripped open to the waist. Ronnie had taken a hammer to the back zipper, rendering it useless. The skirt too was ripped in several places, the fabric sweat-stained.

"My God," Mace muttered. "What...?"

"I'd made him angry."

"So he destroyed your wedding dress. What was he trying to prove?"

"He made me wear it. More times than I can remember."

"Like this?"

She nodded.

"And?"

"And—and then he'd insist on sex."

Mace lifted a section of skirt. "Made access to you easy for him, didn't it?" His eyes darkened from gray to black. "Tell me, Sara. Was sex ever good between the two of you? Was it ever anything except rape?"

Chapter Seven

ଔ

They were back in the sunlight. Sara had stopped shivering, and because she was telling Mace about the flowers she'd grown from seed for her garden, she'd begun to feel like a normal human being again. She hadn't quite shaken off the claustrophobic feeling she'd had while in the mobile. Neither had she come close to believing she'd only imagined Ronnie had been there.

Mace's understanding of flowers was limited to roses and pansies, but he proved to be an enthusiastic student.

"Feel better, do you?" he asked as she pulled the wilted blossoms off a head high foxglove. "I didn't mean to take you back in time, but I needed to know as much as possible."

She stared at him. "You *needed*?"

"Yes."

"Why?"

Instead of answering, he glanced over at the trailer. "I'll get it out of here. Hire someone to haul it off."

"It'll cost—"

"I don't give a damn how much it costs. You need to know it's been destroyed. We both do."

This time she didn't ask for the explanation she knew wouldn't come. "I'm glad," she admitted, "if I had to go in there and bury the ghosts, that you were with me."

"Are they buried?"

No. "I'm working on it."

"You haven't come far enough."

Furious, she whirled on him. "You don't know—"

He hadn't said a word, but his intense gaze stopped her anyway. *Ask him what this is all about. Make him tell you the truth.*

Instead, she went back to deheading her flowers. He watched for a while and then placed his hand over her wrist. She stared at her flesh trapped under his greater strength.

"You hate that," he said. "Being restrained. It's because Ronnie got off on bondage, isn't it?"

Bondage? The word doesn't come close. Try slave, property, possession.

"What else would you like to know?" she demanded. "How he liked sex? He did, frequently and with him always in control."

"Was he into pain?"

A memory curled around her of locked doors and a board positioned between two sawhorses. Naked, arms lashed behind her at the elbows, she straddled the board on tiptoe and begged Ronnie to stop. Instead, he finished tying her ankles together and yanked them back so her aching cunt carried her weight. She screamed and struggled to get her feet under her again, but he continued to grip the rope.

"Don't fight it, Sara," Ronnie had said. *"You know you love it."*

"I don't! I don't! Ronnie, please!"

But he didn't listen. He never had.

Fighting the horrid memory, she forced her surroundings to come back into focus. Mace's fingers held warmth and life. She'd concentrate on those things. "Pain? Sometimes," was all she could say.

"And you put up with it?"

"I was getting a divorce."

"But for a while you—"

"He overwhelmed me, all right!" She remembered cowering in a corner while he came at her with a whip he'd bought at a sex toy shop, how she'd begged him to stop lashing her breasts, belly, and hips—and the tender way he ministered to her flesh when he was done, the silent fuck afterward. "I didn't know how to handle his–his forcefulness and moods."

Mace's look said he didn't understand. "At first his–his take-charge approach, especially in the bedroom, fascinated me. I told myself it was his way of showing me he loved me, something I haven't had much of in my life."

"Your family?"

"My family gave new meaning to the word dysfunctional."

He leaned toward her so she felt his breath on her face. Not just her face, she admitted as moist heat traveled through her. As long as she kept her reaction to herself, she'd be safe—wouldn't she? But maybe it was already too late. Maybe men possessed an instinct telling them when a woman was turned on.

Turned on? What an incredibly freeing and frightening concept.

"Sara, what is it? I said something—"

"No." Words had nothing to do with her body's reaction. A lifetime ago before fear had replaced everything else, she'd responded to the danger that was part and parcel of Ronnie's makeup. Maybe the same thing was happening again. Whatever it was, she'd fight it—wouldn't she?

"You're tense."

"Do you blame me?" she asked. Although she shouldn't, she looked up at him and into his dark, deep eyes. Dizzy, she pressed her free hand against his chest.

He must have misinterpreted because he took control of that hand as well and drew both up and around his neck. He held her in place, her breasts flattened against his chest, bellies touching. She saw nothing except his blurry outline, heard only his beating heart. Could one person's heart somehow enter another's body and take it over?

61

Maybe what she felt had nothing to do with possession. Maybe it was all sexual. God, was it possible Ronnie hadn't destroyed the woman in her after all? Desperate for the answer, she tilted her pelvis toward him.

"Where is Esta?" he whispered.

"In-inside. But she might come out."

"Then we'd better go where she can't see us," he said. He lifted her in his arms and strode toward the barn with its small sleeping room. She didn't fight, didn't utter a word of protest. Instead, she buried her head against his chest and held onto his neck and breathed in his smell. He was in charge—for now. She'd let him direct things—for now.

How can you want this? her own unwanted voice asked. *After everything Ronnie did to you, you can't possibly want a man to possess you.*

* * * * *

The mare and her newborn were both nestled in the hay and sleeping. Sara caught a glimpse of the other pregnant horse as Mace walked toward the room he'd used last night. Then she turned her face toward his chest again and knew only him. She was becoming him, losing herself.

How can you? How can you?

Because I'm tired of being alone.

And when he hurts you?

He won't!

Yes, he will.

Once they were inside the small room, Mace helped her stand. Another wave of dizziness forced her to hold onto his forearms.

He ran his hands along her temples, found the veins pulsing there, and massaged lightly. The sensation raced through her and heated her pussy. "Sara," he whispered. "We both know where this is heading. If you don't want it, leave now. Otherwise…"

"I, ah, I won't run," she told both of them. "I-I need this."

He nodded. "So do I."

They looked at each other for what felt like endless seconds. Her hands had wound up clenched in front of her belly. Memories of when she'd assumed that position in yet more futile attempts to protect herself threatened to surface, but she forced both them and her own voice of caution and warning away.

"Did the two of you ever have sex in here?" Mace asked.

"No. He was allergic to hay. The meds he took to control his reactions made him lethargic so he avoided anywhere hay was stored."

Mace chuckled, and just like that the mood lightened. "Score one for our side." He held out his hands, and she placed hers in them. Her fingers were long and bony, the nails short, hardly the picture of femininity. But next to him, she felt dainty.

"All last night I thought about what would happen if you were in here with me," he told her. "Now that you are, I want to tell you what I'd like to have happen, see if you agree."

Ronnie had never asked what she wanted, and if other men had put the question to her, it had been so long ago she couldn't remember. Her skin felt jumpy, and there wasn't enough air in the small, clean space.

Mace placed her hands on his chest and held them there. Yes, that was his heart beating — and maybe hers too.

"Men don't need much from sex," he whispered.

"I-I wouldn't know."

"It's a well-kept secret, something we don't want women in on. We understand women are more complex so we try to match them by exhibiting as much emotion as we can come up with. But the truth is, give us a good hard fuck and we're happy campers."

"Oh." She sounded like an idiot.

"But fortunately we're more than dogs in heat. At least we can be if we put our minds to it."

She sensed he was deliberately keeping the conversation light. She wanted to thank him, but how could her whole body vibrate when neither of them had so much as removed an article of clothing? Her cunt felt as if it was swelling.

"Anyway, this is what I came up with," he continued. "See if it comes close to your thinking."

"I'll try."

Still holding her hands against him, he moved his free hand to the swell of her buttocks and drew her closer. He began massaging her through her jeans. "First and only rule, we don't talk about anything except us, today."

"Yes, yes."

On the tail of a sigh, he kissed her lightly on the forehead. Her cunt softened and warmed. "As long as we both come, I'm happy."

"Me, come? I don't—"

"You've never had a climax?"

"Of course." She wouldn't tell him that by the end of her so-called marriage, the only climaxes she'd had had been forced from her.

"Good. I just don't want to hear the details because this is the present. The past no longer exists."

"Not now it doesn't," she said and for this moment, she believed herself. "I'd love to climax." Was this her, freely talking about sex with a man—this man?

"But it isn't a given, right?" The pressure on her buttocks increased. She felt the sensation throughout her pelvis. "Not as simple as turning on a light switch?"

"No."

"I figured that. So, here's the plan. I've picked up a few tricks along the way, not all firsthand experience although—

oops, no yesterday."

He pressed the heel of his hand into the small of her back. She sighed and widened her stance before leaning into him. His aroused cock touched her belly. Conditioned to fear a cock, she tensed, then willed herself to relax. It really was an amazing organ, capable of so much change, simple and complex all at once. And what woman wouldn't react to having one in her?

In? Yes.

"We're going to have sex," Mace whispered. "Fuck each other, whatever you want to call it. I think we both knew this from the moment we met."

"I, ah, I wasn't sure but…"

"But what?"

"Let me get used to this, please." She hated her pleading tone. "I've been alone a long time, and before that…"

"This is now."

Although she sensed he was talking to himself as much as her, nothing else could mean more to her. She felt alive today, hungry and frustrated. More and more frequently she'd been masturbating and had taken her need as proof that she was a sexual creature. The thought of having a man satisfy her instead of her own fingers handling the task made her cheeks flame. Her flesh hurt imagining Mace's cock buried deep and full in her, inviting him in instead of having a cock forced on her.

"What are we going to do?" she asked.

Chapter Eight

🕉

Sara stood near the single bed and tried to think what to do with her hands. Mace had already kicked off his shoes. He hooked his thumbs in his waistband and positioned himself in front of her.

"Take my jeans off me," he said. "Put yourself in control."

"I don't feel in control." She held up her trembling hands. Instead of letting her off the hook, he winked. Laughing—actually laughing—she reached for the metal button. She had to concentrate in order to free it, hesitantly took hold of the zipper and pulled down, felt his cock through the fabric.

She couldn't summon the courage to explore him, but somehow her knuckles grazed over the hard, warm mass. By the time she'd unzipped him she was out of breath. Thank goodness for her own practical clothes—except for her braless state that is.

"Not so hard, was it," he observed. "A C+ accomplishment."

"C+? That's all?"

"Sorry, but it didn't do much for me. Oh, the promise was there, but you pretty much left me hanging—or you would have if my cock wasn't already past that point."

He was right. They'd come in here to accomplish something she suspected would change both of them, but so far she hadn't come close to holding up her end of things.

"What do you want me to do?" she asked. She still gripped the zipper between thumb and forefinger.

"I'd say whatever comes naturally, but I'm not sure anything does with you, unfortunately." His expression gentled. "What do you want?"

The question rocked her. "To feel safe," she blurted.

He drew a ragged breath. Alarmed, she leaned back so she could concentrate on his features, but other than a faint darkening to his eyes, she couldn't tell anything. "What?" she demanded.

"I can't promise safe." He ran his rough fingers along her jaw, then touched her throat. She felt the contact from breasts to cunt and turned liquid there.

"Can you at least give me fantasy?" she begged. "The illusion of safe?"

By way of answer, he took her hands and guided them to his waistband. Together they drew jeans and briefs down over his hips and legs. He stepped free of the garments while keeping her hands against his waist. She explored the contour of his navel with her knuckles, tested his pubic hair with her fingertips. He helped her pull his shirt over his head, then bent toward her with his arms outstretched. She focused on black hair charged with electricity.

He drew back and left her holding the last of his clothes. "Study me, Sara. There's nothing here you haven't seen before."

"No, no. There isn't."

"Why don't you tell me what you see?"

Shaking, she struggled to do as he'd asked. She turned her attention to the face she'd already memorized and then to his chest. His shoulders were too wide, the muscles there too strong. She made out the outline of his ribs under tanned flesh and little fat.

"I don't have any hang-ups about my body," he told her. "Whatever you say is all right." Giving emphasis to his words, he stood straight and proud with his arms out from his sides. "Scars, imperfections, even warts—hopefully you can put up with it."

Her lips tingled; a like sensation took hold of her labia

and turned her weak and needy.

"You're—obviously you see your body as a tool," she told him as the mares nickered to each other. "It isn't pretty, but it's strong and functional."

"I never wanted to be pretty."

Laughing eased a little of her tension but didn't quiet the tingling—not that she wanted to be free of the sensation. "I don't see many scars. One along your right upper arm, another thin one over the ribs on that side."

"Courtesy of a horse-training session gone wrong."

"Oh." She stroked his side. As she did, she found a bump in a rib. "You broke that didn't you?"

"And the ones on either side of it. Let's just say letting a twelve-year-old boy drive a tractor down a hill has a tendency to backfire."

"Were you thrown from it, or did it land on you?"

"Spoken like a farm girl. Actually, it was a combination, and in case you're curious, the tractor was in better shape than me. What else, Sara? What more do you need to know about my body?"

What your cock feels like in me. How I'll react to your weight over mine. "I, ah, this makes me uncomfortable."

"I don't exactly feel in control." He indicated his naked body with its blood-swollen cock straining toward her. "But this is what you need, to see me as vulnerable." His hands became fists.

"You, vulnerable? Never."

"Yes, me, vulnerable." He lifted a fist toward her, but although she'd shrunk from the weapon countless times in the past, she stood her ground. Gentle and firm at the same time, he pressed his fist against her breastbone. "Sara, you have no idea—no idea what it took for me to present myself naked to you."

A gift. He was gifting her with his body. Fighting tears, she slowly, reverently closed her hands around his cock. She'd sometimes fantasized about amputating Ronnie's cock, but Mace's felt different, was different.

"What?" he asked. "You're just standing there holding…"

Embarrassed, she started to release him. He stopped her by covering her hands with his own. "What were you thinking?"

"It…has nothing to do with us." *Please.* "Are you sure you want…?"

"Want, yes. As for anything approaching sanity, that's something else entirely." His jaw muscles clenched. "What do you need me to do to you?"

"I'm, ah, I'm not used to having a say in what happens."

"The bastard. The goddamn bastard."

"Mace, don't, please. It-it doesn't matter. He'd dead." *Please, let him stay dead.*

"Do you want me to handle things?" he asked.

No, her brain screamed. "Yes," she said.

"All right." He drew her hands off his cock and positioned them so her arms were out from her side, her elbows stiff, her fingers aching to touch him again. He reached for her jeans' fastening, but although she hated herself, she couldn't stop the backward step.

"Don't." His voice was thick with warning. "Don't move unless I tell you to. And don't speak until I give you permission."

Wait for permission. She understood that, oh God did she! Sweat broke out under her breasts and in the small of her back, and she trembled. But although those reactions had been part of what passed for sex between her and Ronnie, the wet heat in her pussy wasn't. Closing herself off from the undeniable fear, she focused on her body's reaction to Mace Seeger's hands and eyes.

He wasted no time pulling her jeans and panties down as

far as her shoes would allow. Then he told her to sit on the bed, and she did, her fingers gripping the cheap spread. He knelt before her and lifted first one foot and then the other onto his thigh so he could untie her laces. When he'd removed her shoes, he drew out the act of pulling off her socks and jeans and panties.

"Scoot to the edge of the bed," he said. Still shaking, she did as he commanded. Breathing took effort.

"Spread your legs."

"I—" Well-trained in obedience, she clenched her teeth and waited. Instead of slapping her or pulling on her labial lips as Ronnie would have done, Mace began stroking the inside of her thighs. Just like that, her muscles felt as if they were disappearing, oozing out of her, and although he hadn't given her permission to move, she repositioned her hands behind her and leaned back, increasing his access to her. She hated the feel of cotton on her upper body.

Mace began with butterfly-wing touches near her knees. Then his fingertips danced closer to her cunt, the journey slow and erratic. He used a light touch with his nails to create tiny circles and curves on her sensitive flesh. Wet heat boiled up inside her, built at the entrance to her vagina, then spilled out.

"There's the reaction I was looking for," he muttered. "Being able to turn you on says something about…"

About what? She ached to ask but he'd commanded her to remain silent. His forefingers tapped at the entrance to her cave and then retreated. On fire, she lifted her pelvis toward him. Instead of taking her offering, he pressed the heel of his hand against her mons.

All at once, she was aware of nothing except how trapped and empty and starved her cunt felt. Her clit ached.

"Look at yourself," he commanded. "Look at what I'm doing to you."

She struggled to straighten. By the time she'd found her balance, he'd run a forefinger inside her. He continued to press down on her mons; at the same time, he rocked the heel of his hand back and forth. His buried forefinger explored her wet depths, touching here, there, everywhere.

No matter how she struggled to do as he'd said, she couldn't get a clear look at herself. Now not only was his hand on her muff in the way, but her vision kept blurring.

"What do you see, Sara?"

"I…your hand."

"That's right. My hand on and in you. It's what you want, isn't it? For your body to become my playground, for me to take over."

I don't know; I've never known. "What-what do you want me to say?"

He changed position so his whole palm covered her mons. He began a twisting movement and still pressed with enough strength that it bordered on the painful. A second finger joined the one inside her.

Invasion! With a small cry, she tried to pull him off her but lost the support her hand had provided and started to fall back. She struggled to straighten.

"No, Sara. Later, you can have a say in what happens, but not now." He punctuated his remark by pushing her against the bed.

Panting and too close to terror, she stared at the ceiling. His hand was already back on her mons. The other continued to concern itself with her pussy.

Old mental tapes of having to submit to her husband's fascination with bondage started to play. She lost the distinction between Ronnie and Mace and knew all too well what would happen—ropes, a collar, nipple clamps, her begging and him laughing.

The tapes slowed, stopped. At first she couldn't make sense of the change, but bit-by-bit her body spelled out the difference. The hands on and in her sex weren't rough and uncaring but gentle. Mace's fingers kissed her clit, caressed her

71

labia, stroked her urethra even. Sensations came one after another, waves of feeling that increased her self-lubrication and turned her nipples into hot, hard rocks. She scooted toward him and spread her legs even more.

She tried to make sense of what he was doing, to find some kind of rhythm or pattern, but he kept changing direction. In a disjoined way she understood this was how he intended to control what she felt and experienced, but she didn't care. He'd taken over her body. Maybe she'd freely relinquished responsibility for herself, not that it mattered.

God, the way it felt when he ran a nail over her so-sensitive clit! If he kept it up—please!—she'd climax.

Climax? Had she ever willingly had one or had they always been forced from her traitorous body?

Fear bit at her again, and she struggled to keep on top of it. By the time she'd convinced herself that Ronnie Parmenter wasn't here, Mace was no longer playing with her sex. She felt her body roll toward his as he joined her on the bed. He was on his knees. His knees pressed against her hip.

She started to reach for him—for his cock, but he captured her wrists and drew her hands over her head. After crossing one wrist over the other, he pressed down lightly, then did the same to the undersides of her arms as if locking her in place.

"Remember the rules," he said as she struggled not to close her eyes against his intense gaze. "No movement or talking unless I say so."

I'll try. I just can't promise.

"Do you understand why I'm doing this?"

Afraid to so much as twitch, she returned his stare. She felt unbelievably alive, scared and turned-on, submissive and yet somehow in control—different from the way Ronnie had always made her feel.

"You know your role, don't you? Better than I do that's for damn sure. I've never tried bondage with a woman. Fantasized about it but..."

He continued to regard her while she fought the weight of her inner demons. Pressure continued to build in her cunt. If she didn't clench her teeth and hold her breath, she'd have begged him to spear her. She'd been left wanting so many times. She should know how to deal with the frustration, but Mace was new, the unknown, danger and promise and a huge, hard cock.

"Maybe I shouldn't have done what I just did, playing with you," Mace said as he began unbuttoning her shirt. He continued to watch her hands—to hold her whole body in place with his hot gaze. "But I wanted to know how responsive you are."

Too responsive. Maybe that's why I stayed with Ronnie as long as I did.

"You're a hot woman, Sara." He finished with the last button and pulled the shirt open, exposing her breasts. "I don't want to get burned." He nestled a nipple between thumb and forefinger, increased his grip, and drew it upward. "That's what I kept telling myself—don't get close to the fire." He rolled the nub back and forth. The sensation flowed over her belly to her crotch. Hotter and hotter, it licked at her clit. Panting, she ground her ass into the mattress.

"What are you, Sara? Fire and flame? Where do you come from, heaven or hell? Where are you taking me—taking us?"

Chapter Nine

ജ

Sara only dimly comprehended that Mace had asked a question. Maybe she could have concentrated if he hadn't grabbed her around the waist and scooted her further onto the bed. After pressing on her wrists to remind her of her invisible bonds, he spread her legs more before positioning himself on his knees between them. She couldn't stop trembling.

"What is this?" He rested his hands on her inner thighs, his fingers stroking in tune with the slight vibrations. "Anticipation, Sara? You aren't afraid of me, are you?"

Yes, a little. Mostly I'm afraid of being out-of-control.

"Don't answer," he told her although she had no intention of revealing any more than she already had. "I don't want to hear it—not yet anyway."

He rocked back to give himself a clearer view of her sex organs. Although she'd never studied herself while aroused, she knew her clit grew and hardened, a secret organ wantonly exposed. It had to be blood red and wet with her body's juices.

To her consternation, he spread her labial lips and bathed them with the fluid she readily supplied. Staring at the ceiling, she could only imagine how close his cock was to her cunt, but her raging mind supplied the fantasy. First he'd toy with her by touching his tip to her drenched opening. She'd scoot closer, suck him in, provide a home for his sex organ. Her pussy muscles would close down around him, and he'd know what it felt like to be trapped and helpless, on fire, burning. Laughing with power, she'd milk him and turn his cock into a pumping machine. He'd grunt and sweat. His muscles would strain, thrusts coming faster, stronger. She'd ride him, ride him, ride—

A cattle prod couldn't have shocked her more. One moment she was deep in fantasy. The next, he'd run something—maybe a fingernail—over her clit. A climax surged over her. Not just her pussy but her whole body felt trapped in the tidal wave heating her, taking her higher, higher.

Her breath whistled. She heard herself cry out, the sob long and guttural. Sweat coated her belly and between her breasts but most of the wetness came from her cunt. She smelled her sex-scent and felt her clit jerk and tremble. The sheer wonder of her sexuality rocked her. Wild with equal amounts of disbelief and joy, she surrendered. She kept sobbing, legs beating a helpless tattoo.

She became aware of his hand pressing against her belly. He'd slid his other hand under her ass so his forefinger was now between her cheeks and just touching her anus. He increased both pressures, holding her climax between his hands, drawing it out, giving it nowhere to go except flowing through her veins. Drenched and spent, she dissolved into the mattress but continued to come.

And come.

* * * * *

"You're crying."

"No, I'm not."

Mace leaned over her and lowered his body so his cock and chest brushed flesh that felt sandpapery. He licked away one tear and then another. Sara wrapped her arms around his neck and held him against her. If he hadn't supported his weight on his elbows, he would have crushed her, but she didn't care. Was she responsible for all this sweat, or did some of it come from him?

"Crying isn't a crime, Sara," he whispered with his mouth so close to hers maybe they were breathing the same air. "Don't be ashamed of it."

She still half believed she'd just finished a race and couldn't get her mind to hold onto anything except his body. "I never let myself cry. It's too dangerous."

"Why?"

"He uses — he uses my weakness against me."

"He's dead, Sara. Dead."

Bitch! Whore! You belong to me.

Terrified, Sara tried to sit up, but Mace's body held her in place. "What is it?" His tone was soothing, an essential contact with reality.

"No-nothing."

"Don't lie," he insisted. She forced herself to stop struggling but couldn't begin to relax. "What is it? I came on too strong."

"No. No. I, ah, I needed...loved coming." If she kept her eyes open, maybe whatever now shared the room with them couldn't take over. "I, ah, it's my turn. Tell me what you want me to do to you."

He rolled off her and propped himself up on an elbow. After staring at her breasts for a moment, he placed his free hand over the breast closest to him. "Do whatever you want. I'll love it."

Post-climax weakness still held her muscles. If it wasn't for the fear nibbling at her nerve endings, she could have put her mind to responding to his needs, couldn't she? In an attempt to put distance between herself and what she knew she hadn't imagined hearing, she stroked Mace's chest.

Don't! I'm warning you, whore. You don't touch anyone except me. Ever.

Beyond terror, Sara struggled to her hands and knees and scooted as far as she could from Mace. Her shirt still clung to her shoulders.

"Sara! What is it?"

"He's here. Watching us."

"Who?"

"Ronnie."

That's right, bitch. Your husband, lord, and master.

"No!" she screamed. "No, you aren't! You're dead, Ronnie. Dead."

"Sara." Mace grabbed her, and although she struggled to keep distance between herself and the man responsible for her first freely experienced climax, he refused to let go. After a moment, she sagged against him.

"What happened?" Mace whispered as he nestled her head on his chest and stroked her hair. "Tell me."

"I-It'll sound insane."

"Listen to me, Sara." His words spread over her and reminded her of the way he'd gifted her with a climax. "I've spent enough time around you to know you aren't crazy. I *need* to understand."

The word *need* seemed to have been wrenched from him, and she straightened so she could study him. Instead of amusement or disbelief, he had a wary, resigned air about him. He was, she realized, a man determined to face what he had to.

"You aren't surprised, are you?" she asked. "Did you think something like this was going to happen?"

"What happened?"

Tell him, bitch. Tell the stud to keep his hands off my woman. Otherwise, he's a dead man.

"Mace!" Her voice shook. "Leave! Now!" She shoved, nearly knocking him off the bed.

"No," he said and reached for her again.

More afraid than she'd been even when Ronnie choked her, she evaded Mace and scrambled to her feet. She clutched her shirttail and tried to cover her pubic area with it.

"He's here. He's talking to me."

Mace stood, clenched his fists, and looked around. "Damn you, you bastard," he ordered. "Leave us alone!"

Sara vaguely comprehended that he'd included himself in his order. Out of the corner of her eye, she spotted a candle on a wooden crate. The candle served as emergency light but she'd never used it because of the fire danger. She grabbed it and the nearby lighter. Her hands shook, but she managed to light the candle and hold it aloft.

"Do you see this, Ronnie? Touch Mace, hurt him in any way, and I'll burn down the barn. I swear I will."

"Sara! What are you—?"

"Don't try to stop me," she warned. "Ronnie, this isn't a bluff." The flickering light gave her strength. The thought of throwing the candle into a pile of hay made her feel like Superwoman. "I'll kill the horses, burn myself to death. Then what will you do?"

Bitch! Whore!

"You'll be alone, Ronnie. You loved the horses, even suffered with allergies to hay. You never cared about a human being, but you loved the horses." The idea of trapping the two mares and their babies inside a blazing barn made her sick, but she couldn't stop. "You worked on this barn," she went on. "The only thing you touched here." She waved the candle from side to side. "You were proud of what you'd done. I have the power to destroy that. I mean it. You'll have to listen to the horses screaming and know you're responsible."

I'll kill you, you bitch!

Was there something dark and heavy in the room? If there was more to Ronnie than this voice inside her— "You can't kill anything, Ronnie," she insisted although she remembered cruel hands around her throat. "You're dead. Someone did what I prayed I had the courage to do. They killed you. I'm free, alive. You hate it because my body no longer belongs to you, but you can't do anything about it." She swept the candle within a few inches of the tangled coverlet, then brought it near her hair. "It's my body now, Ronnie. My life."

Something slammed into her and sent her flying onto the bed. Someone yanked the candle out of her hand.

"Sara, no!"

Bitch!

As a wild-eyed Mace blew out the candle, she scrambled onto her hands and knees. "What are you doing?" she demanded. "It's the only way I can stop him."

"Are you insane?"

"If I am, it's because he made me that way."

I'll kill you, Sara. Slow. And I'll laugh the whole time.

"Give me the candle," she demanded. She launched herself at Mace. He stiff-armed her, the heel of his hand connecting with her jaw. Stars exploded behind her eyes, and she felt herself start to sag.

More stars appeared. Her teeth felt loose, and her legs refused to hold her. The last thing she was aware of was Mace's naked chest against her fingers.

Chapter Ten

Shocked, Mace held Sara in his arms. The heel of his hand throbbed from connecting with her chin, but that was nothing compared to what she must have felt. He'd started to roll her onto the bed so he could better check her breathing when her eyes opened.

"I'm sorry." He'd never meant anything more. "I didn't mean—God, I never intended to hurt you."

She tentatively touched her chin.

"I was just trying to stop you," he explained. He longed to shelter her but wasn't sure what he should do.

She blinked several times as if trying to make sense of his words. Then her gaze became steady. Lying there small and helpless and naked should have kicked his libido into overdrive, but he couldn't stop thinking about her frenzied actions just before he'd accidentally knocked her out.

"You were fighting Ronnie, weren't you?" Icy fingers chased down his spine.

"Yes," she whimpered and tried to sit up. "He won't die! Why won't he stay dead?"

Because I'm here.

"I don't know," he said because he didn't dare voice the truth. "Sara, you have to get away from here. Living like this isn't healthy. You've got to start over, live your own life."

She stared at him with such hunger he hurt for her. "I know, but I can't leave Esta and Jerome."

"I understand." It was the last thing he wanted to say. "But if he kills you…" *What was he saying?!*

Scooting around, she planted her feet on the ground and stood. She swayed a little, then dressed in a businesslike manner. "He won't kill me," she said with her back to him. "Not as long as he believes he can go on torturing me."

* * * * *

Mace waited until Sara had gone to help Esta before retrieving his cell phone from Ronnie's car where he'd left it plugged into the ashtray.

His sister answered after the third ring. "Where are you?" Judi demanded. "I've been trying to reach you."

"How are you?" he asked instead of answering.

"All right, I guess. You know that temporary agency I filled out an application with? I have an interview with them tomorrow for a part-time job."

"You'll do great." He hoped he sounded convincing. "Just keep your fingers limber and you'll ace their typing tests."

"At least I have one marketable skill, one that hopefully will keep me out of bars."

He should be there. Damn it, his only sister needed him. But the woman he'd just given a climax to needed him more. "Sis, I'm going to be gone for awhile. I wish I could say how long, but I can't. Maybe in a couple of days—"

"Where are you?"

A few months ago Judi had been so emotionally fragile that he'd kept everything from her, but she was getting stronger, at least that's what he told himself. "In Harney County, Oregon."

"Oregon? Please, no."

"I had to," he said although he still didn't fully understand what had compelled him to come here. "It's about closure. Judi, I've met Parmenter's adoptive parents. They're good and decent people."

"No."

"Listen to me. Everything's all right." *Liar.* "They're getting up in years. I'm going to help them get their place fixed up so they can sell it." He listed some of the things that needed doing so she wouldn't break in and beg him to return. "They don't know who I am. Not really."

"No," Judi whimpered. "Mace, please."

"You're all right, sis. Strong. Look, I'll call tomorrow night, and you can tell me how the interview went. What about the electric bill? The money I gave you covered it, didn't it?"

* * * * *

Jerome looked surprised when Mace suggested they begin work on the farm by getting rid of unused items.

"I agree," Jerome said, "the place looks like a refuge for discarded equipment, but this isn't your responsibility. Offering to help me with the roof is beyond generous." He frowned at his deformed hand. "I'll hire some men to lend a hand with the rest."

He'd deliberately approached Jerome out by the cattle-loading chute where Sara couldn't hear. "You're not going to get rid of me that easy," he said, winking. "In case you haven't noticed, I'm taken with Sara. I hope it doesn't bother you, her being your daughter-in-law."

Jerome frowned. "What about your own job? Them trees ain't going to harvest themselves."

"Harvest isn't for a couple more months, and my foreman can handle what little needs to be done now. Jerome, it isn't right for her to stay here; you know it."

"No, it isn't right." Jerome stuck out his hand for a shake. "This is between you and me," he said. "Esta never did see Ronnie for what he was. Not having children of her own, well, I think you know what I mean. But Sara never looked at Ronnie the way Esta looks at me even after all these years. When Ronnie was a boy I could hold him down when he lost his temper, which happened a lot. Then he became a teenager, and I couldn't control him." He shook his head. "The truth, I didn't want Sara marrying him. She's such a sweet, gentle thing."

You haven't seen her aroused — or terrified.

"I was afraid Ronnie would run over her. Sometimes I saw signs he'd — that he'd hurt her. Now he's dead and I want things to be good for her." Jerome squared on him. "Go ahead, court her. But if you hurt her, you'll have to answer to me."

If you hurt her, rang through Mace's mind. God knows it was the last thing he wanted to do, but what if he couldn't help it?

* * * * *

"You what?" Sara managed.

"It's what you want. It has to be."

Mace was right. Almost nothing meant more than never having to look at the hated mobile home again. But to know it was being hauled away tomorrow left her in disbelief. It was approaching dusk, and she should be helping Esta with dinner, but although she'd spent the day avoiding Mace, she'd also wanted to know what he and Jerome had been up to. She'd also needed to hear his voice and feel his impact on her skin. Now they were in the barn watching for signs that the other pregnant mare was going into labor.

"You're upset because I didn't consult you before making the arrangements," Mace said. He'd been on the roof for several hours where wind and sun had attacked his hair. While Ronnie had always had a pasty appearance because he spent so much time in his rig or in a bar, everything about Mace said he embraced nature.

"Yes I am," she said although she wasn't sure why she felt so unnerved. Was being near the man she'd nearly fucked and ached to do so again the only reason? "Don't do my thinking for me. Despite the way I've acted, I'm not crazy."

"I've seen crazy. Believe me, you aren't close."

"You have? When?"

"Doesn't matter." He wiped sweat off his forehead, then touched the side of her neck. "I think you should be gone when it happens. You don't need to watch it being hauled away."

Gone. Out of her life and soul. Buried with Ronnie.

"Why so fast?" she asked. "Did…did Jerome think this was a priority?"

"He agrees it's a good idea, but it's *my* priority, Sara." He ran a finger over her ear, catching her on fire. "I can't make sense of what's going on around us, and I don't believe you can either."

When she shook her head—no easy task with his fingers on her throat again—he slipped closer. "Sara, you were a victim for too long. It's time to let Ronnie know he no longer has any control over you."

I want to believe! Oh, how I want to believe.

Even as she prayed, she sensed darkness and weight. No! She'd given her body to Mace under this roof and in doing so had exorcised Ronnie. He couldn't have her back, he couldn't!

"What is it?" Mace demanded. "You're so tense."

"I don't understand what he's doing," she said. She placed Mace's hand over her breast. This was reality! Life. Living.

"Is he here?"

She closed her eyes and leaned into her lover. "He's trying."

Chapter Eleven

&

Over her weak protests, Mace had carried her out of the barn and to a nearby group of cottonwood trees. He hadn't put her down until they were in the middle of them and might not have even then if she hadn't assured him she and Ronnie had never had sex here.

Her skin felt as if fireflies danced on it, soft and weightless creatures who touched her flesh with heat. Mace hadn't asked permission before removing her clothes, and it hadn't occurred to her to resist. She stood naked before him as the sun set, bathing them in soft orange and red. Esta and Jerome might come looking for them. She should—should what?

"It's all right," Mace said as if reading her mind. "Jerome and I had a man-to-man talk. He understands. He'll explain things to Esta."

"Why are we doing this?" she asked although she already knew the only thing she needed to—she and Mace were going to have sex.

"Because it's what we want."

He'd made no move to remove his clothing. Just the same, she felt her strength, her power over this man.

"I-I thought about you all day," she admitted with her hands by her sides, her nipples so hard they hurt, and her cunt already hot and wet. "About wanting you inside me."

"Was it good?"

"Very good." She laughed. "You're an incredible lover—at least in my mind you are."

He rested a hand on her hip. The touch spread outward

until she swore she felt him everywhere. She'd gift him with her body. Free and open in ways she'd barely dreamed of, she'd present herself to him to handle as a man handles a woman he respects, maybe even loves.

Love. The word held no meaning to her, but she didn't fear it. Instead, it gave her the strength to take his hand and guide it between her legs.

"Just like that?" he asked. "You're sure."

"Yes." The air smelled of grass and bark. A few crickets had begun their night song. Although the breeze was slight, it rattled the leaves. She couldn't remember seeing a more vibrant sunset or her cunt feeling more alive.

"I have a fantasy," he said and lifted a leg so it hooked over his hip. He wrapped an arm around her waist, lifted her, and backed her against the nearest tree. With her back supported by the tree and the hand on her leg doing the same, he bent toward her so his jeans scraped her belly and thighs. "We're at a spa, one of those expensive things that smell of flowers and have soft music and muted light."

She'd never been to such a place, but she could imagine — and revel in the feel of air on her labia and clit. Hanging onto his neck, she waited for him to play out his fantasy.

"We're the only people there." He kissed one eyelid and then the other. "The owners knew we needed to be alone." The hand not on her thigh slipped toward her sex. She struggled to concentrate on what he was saying.

"The spa overlooks the ocean. The windows are open, and we smell an approaching storm." He shifted position and worked his hand closer to the part of her that existed only for him. She loved being nude! Loved it! "There's a high, narrow bed covered with a satin sheet." He ran the back of his thumb over her labia, forcing a sob from her. Still, she managed to keep hold of his neck and press her back against the tree, increasing his access to her.

"You stand near the bed, running your hand over the

86

satin. I know your skin will feel like satin so I slip off your clothes." His nail skimmed her clit, and she rose onto her toes.

"I pick you up and place you on the bed on your stomach." Again his nail caressed her clit. She sighed. Her stomach tightened. "You stretch out with your face turned toward me but your eyes closed. I spread your legs, take some lavender-scented lotion and rub it over your calves, the back of your knees, your thighs."

When he touched her clit for the third time, she prayed he'd claim it, but he simply slid over it before entering her vagina.

"You try to turn over so I can see your sex, but I won't let you." He buried his forefinger in her. "Do you understand what I'm saying, Sara? In this fantasy, I do to you what we both want."

A cramp in the leg supporting her weight wrenched her from the fantasy. Yelping, she pulled free and crouched so she could massage her calf. Even as she fought the pain, her awareness of her sexual excitement had her a breath away from massaging her pussy. He stroked her head as she released the knot in her muscle. Then he helped her stand.

"I want to do something to you," he said. Because it wasn't quite dark, she could make out his features. His dark gaze fascinated her, but didn't frighten her.

"What?" She tried to reach for his shirt buttons, but he pushed her away, then took hold of her wrists.

"Another kind of fantasy, one I think you need."

"A more lavish spa?"

He chuckled, then turned serious again. "No. Not this time. Do you trust me?"

"I, ah, I don't know how to answer."

"No, I don't imagine you do. All right." Slowly, letting her anticipate everything he was doing, he positioned her hands above her head and flattened them against the tree. "How does that feel?"

Ronnie had imprisoned her like this, only he'd used ropes and chains. "All right."

"Good. It won't go further than this, tonight."

Tonight. When he released her hands, she remained as he'd placed her.

"Good," he repeated. "Tell me something. Did Ronnie perform cunnilingus on you?"

Icy fingers marched over her flesh. Her sex felt frozen, yet hot beneath the cold. "He, ah, you mean with his mouth?"

"Yes."

She waited through the worst of her reaction before answering. "He, ah, he did what he called stimulating the cunt, but never with his mouth."

"What did he use?"

"Mace, please." She started to move, but he stopped her with a look.

"I'm sorry," he said. "I shouldn't have asked, at least not yet."

Before she could decide whether to ask for an explanation, he dropped to his knees before her. Resting his hands over her hips, he leaned forward. Scared and excited all at once, she waited for his next move. She jumped when he ran his tongue over her belly, then made herself stand still. She tried to relax, but how could she when—oh my!

The last of her fear melted away. She knew nothing, cared nothing except for the sweet and wonderful feel of his tongue in her navel. The sensation flowed out and deep but mostly down. Over and over again, he pushed his tongue into her navel, sometimes the touch light, other times possessive. She barely remembered to keep her hands above her, and every time she tried to look down at him, she lost control over the muscles in her neck, causing her head to fall forward. Finally she leaned against the tree and simply experienced.

Maybe he'd never grow tired of her belly button. She

loved the way his tongue felt on that seldom-touched part of her anatomy and might have been content if he hadn't ignited countless nerves throughout her sex. He must know about the growing heat and dampness there because he turned his attention to her belly and hipbones, her pelvis. She struggled to keep her hips from moving. Then he buried his face in her pubic hair and bathed her mons in damp heat, and she gave up.

He was so gentle, his caresses loving. She sensed him settling himself on his ass and waited—alive—for what he planned to do next. When he ran his hands between her legs and widened her stance, she opened herself even further.

Then he closed his hands over her buttocks and pulled her hips toward him, and she imagined her sex organs opening up to him like a spring flower. If he didn't like what he saw—

He did! The first touch of tongue over her labia lifted her onto her toes. He stopped, and she lowered herself again, but then he found the entrance to her vagina, and she once more thought she'd levitate.

More times than she could begin to count, he stroked her clitoris and perineum. He isolated her clitoral hood, inner and outer lips, the vagina opening itself. When he reached the entrance to her womb, he announced his presence with the tip of his tongue. He followed that with a long, hot kiss, then brought the blade of his tongue into play. Only once did memories of other ways she'd been stimulated there enter her mind, but she shook off what had been a nightmare and lived in the moment.

Mace's touch changed constantly, keeping her interest at fever pitch trying to anticipate what he'd do next. She never knew whether he'd focus on her vagina or nearly throw her into the heavens by kissing the space between her genitals and anus.

"Good?" he asked between licks.

"Good!" she all but screamed.

Her pussy felt as if it was liquefying, and although some part of her knew she was drenching both of them, she didn't care. She floated. She felt grounded. He played the tune and she danced for him.

Awareness of the rest of her body, specifically her breasts, surfaced. She'd disobeyed his order to keep her hands over her head by massaging the swollen mounds, but she couldn't help herself. Everything flowed together—cunt and breasts linked by sensation. Her cunt wept, laughed, shouted.

Then her pelvis jerked, and she came. Came! He'd stopped stimulating her but still gripped her hips and rode with her. Her breath whistled and snagged. She heard herself cry out; the sound went on and on, a dam released. Ripples of fire and electricity pulsed through her pussy.

And when her legs gave out and she slumped to the ground, he was there to catch her.

* * * * *

"Don't you want—?" Sara began, but Mace silenced her by placing his hand over her mouth.

"Not now," he said and helped her sit up. As a child he'd held some mercury in his palm, rolling it one way and then the other. Although Sara had come back to earth, she still reminded him of that viscous liquid. And like the mercury, she shimmered.

"We have to go back," he told her. "I wanted it to be like this, for you."

She tried to say something, but he wouldn't let her. "When you go to bed tonight, I want you to think about what happened, to know there are men who put their woman's needs before their own."

He wondered if she'd respond to the word *their*, but if she'd noticed, she gave no indication. Oblivious to the less than soft ground under her buttocks, she remained nestled against him. After several seconds, she pushed her tongue against his palm.

"Can I talk now?" she asked.

"I've never known a woman who can't."

Slapping him gently on the cheek, she laughed. "That was incredible."

"You never—"

"Not like that. Wow! In a word, wow!"

"So you think you might want to do it again?"

By way of answer, she took hold of his swollen cock through his jeans. "Oh, I think so. The question is, can you handle being left in this condition?"

Hearing her joke lightened his heart. He kissed her long and hard, and she gave as good as he did. "I'm not sure," he admitted. "I'll survive for now, but the next time—"

"When?" she asked.

"Soon," he promised. "Soon."

She must have taken him at his word because she hummed as she went about putting her clothes back on. Even in the afterglow of her climax, he couldn't completely shake off the reason behind his decision to gift her. Not only did she need to be brought fully to life but so did the monster who'd given both of them a taste of hell.

Now you really have a reason to hate me, he told Ronnie. *A reason to pit your strength against mine.*

Chapter Twelve

એડ

They'd spent the evening in the ranch house with Esta and Jerome because Esta had needed to talk about how hard it would be to leave the place where she'd spent so many years and how much she looked forward to moving into a new house.

Although she wasn't sure Mace wanted to hear about Esta's plans, hopes, and fears, Sara hadn't tried to change the subject. Fortunately, Esta had put a casserole in the oven by the time she and Mace walked in. She'd been able to slip into the bathroom for a badly needed shower and had thrown on a little makeup to tone down her flushed cheeks. She hadn't trusted herself to sit near Mace.

Now Jerome was yawning and telling his wife they needed to get some sleep if they were going to be ready for the realtor who'd agreed to stop by tomorrow. Either Jerome's yawns or her own earlier exertions had caught up with her because suddenly Sara could barely keep her eyes open.

"We all need some sleep," Mace announced as he headed toward the door. "Busy day tomorrow." Then he looked over his shoulder at her.

If you need me, he mouthed. *Call.*

* * * * *

"You're mine."

"No, I'm not! Ronnie, you don't own – "

"Shut up, bitch!"

Fear rumbled through Sara as Ronnie backed her into a corner. She didn't know how he'd managed to tie her hands behind her or what had happened to her clothing. Terror knotted her belly at the look in his eyes and lengths of rope slung over his shoulder. She tried to run past him, but he grabbed her around the neck and yanked her against him. She fought and tried to scream. The sound strangled first in her throat and then into the gag he shoved into her mouth. After knotting the rag behind her head, he slammed her breasts-first into the trailer's metal wall. Holding her in place with an elbow jammed into her back, he easily, expertly tied a rope around her neck.

She whimpered when he looped the end of the rope through a hook in the ceiling and tightened it so she had to stand on tiptoe, her head to one side.

"That's how it's going to be tonight, cunt," her husband said. "My way for as long as I want it."

Oh god, she knew what was coming – and couldn't do a thing about it. Still, when he came at her with the nipple clamps, she whirled this way and that. Laughing, he kept jabbing the clamps at her until she lost her footing. By the time she'd regained her balance and no longer felt as if she was choking, he'd tightened the clamps around both nipples.

"My latest toys," he informed her. He grabbed hold of the ring attached to one clamp and used it to draw her breast toward him. "Picked this up during my last run to Frisco. Guaranteed to put new sizzle in bondage play – that's what the package said. Only we aren't playing, are we, bitch?"

Nausea rose in her throat. She nearly wet herself.

When he pulled a slender chain out of his back pocket, she simply stared at it. Where could she go? What could she do? Feeling like a piece of meat instead of a human being, she shook and begged for mercy with her eyes as he fastened the chain to the nipple rings. It dangled nearly to her waist between her breasts until he grabbed the chain and pulled it toward him.

"Effective, ain't it?" He laughed. "Two boobs for the price of one." He gathered up more of the length until she felt as if her breasts were being torn from her. She had no choice but to step as close to him as the noose allowed.

"Now, the thing is – " his tone was conversational. "Knowing

my whore of a wife the way I do, a little breast torture isn't going to get you off." He pulled up, then down, sending hot fingers of pain through her. "Hmm. Wonder if I can get my money back for this defective merchandise." He increased the downward pressure. "Nah, ain't the toy that's defective, it's my cunt-wife."

Tears streamed down her cheeks. She could barely see.

"But I'm not a man who gives up easy, not at all." His grin said he was proud of himself. "Trial and error, trial and error."

After a sharp yank, he released the chain. The pain had barely subsided when she realized he'd stepped behind her and had started to slide something between her legs. Beyond reason, she tried to kick back at him, but the rope around her neck stopped her.

Whatever he'd touched her with slid lower and lower on her right leg, looped around it, cinching tight around her ankle. The noose didn't allow her to see, but she knew he'd tied her to the foot of the bed.

"Can't kick me now, can you bitch?" Proving his point, he stroked her hip, her ass, her thigh. When he ran his hand between her legs and raked his thumbnail over her labia, she sobbed into the gag.

"Ah, my devoted wife wants her loving husband to perform his husbandry duties, does she? Well, I would." He pushed her labia aside and shoved two fingers into her vagina. "But the hell of it is, straight sex doesn't get my wife off. She needs me to be creative." His fingers started to retreat, then rammed deeper, in her mind, she kicked with all her strength. In reality, she could do nothing.

"Ah." He wiggled his invading fingers. "Least she's getting wet. Don't worry sweetie. Don't worry."

He was no longer finger-fucking her. Despite everything she knew about her husband, blind relief washed over her.

Then he stood in front of her, a riding crop gripped in his right hand. He stroked her between the breasts with it. "See, I brought yet another toy for us to play with." He snapped the short whip in the air. "I love that sound. Bet you do too."

She couldn't think, couldn't breath.

"Ah sweetie." Almost tenderly, he closed his hand around her chin and held her so she had to look him in the eye. "I'm not going to

beat you. You know I wouldn't damage the merchandise. Fortunately, I've figured out a way to use this – " he again cracked the whip, "*without leaving scars.*"

He released her chin and took hold of the nipple chain. The crop handle slid between her legs. Her cunt noted the tightly wrapped leather, the ungiving wooden base beneath, the warmth from where he'd been holding it.

"*The thing is –* " he pulled on the chain. At the same time, he began a sawing motion with the crop handle. "*I'm giving you a lot to concentrate on.*" He pushed the handle tight against her cunt and continued moving it back and forth. "*But in the end, you're going to thank me for it. Breasts and pussy, they're all erogenous zones.*" He dragged down on the chain. "*Having all this going on at once gotta make for a better climax.*"

I don't want this, she tried to tell him but of course, she couldn't speak. Still, she cursed him in her mind. *If she could kill him right now, she would.*

Instead, because Ronnie knew her in ways she hated, she responded to his manipulations. The clamps on her breasts hurt, but the sensation between her legs and against her sex was different – beyond all reason erotic. She had a sex drive, damn it – triggers waiting beneath the surface and needing to be pushed.

His smile didn't reach his eyes. "*Softening you up, that's what I'm doing my dear wife. Getting you ready for the real thing*" The strokes against her pussy became longer, slower, deeper. She was losing herself in the sensation, juices letting down and betraying her.

He removed the handle and fingered it. Then he released the chain and ran his fingers over her hot, wet folds. "*Look at that.*" He showed her his drenched fingers. "*The little lady loves what her husband is doing for her. It'd be a shame to deny her her wifely reward, a damn shame.*"

The predatory look in his eyes stripped the strength from her muscles and briefly took her away from her panting need for sexual release. "*Yeah, I'll give you your reward all right, let you get off this time.*" He slid the handle between her legs again. The end rested at the entrance to her vagina. "*But you gotta see it from my position.*" Smile fading, he spun the end past her lips and into her. "*Why should you have all the fun? Has to be good for me too – good as I can make it."*

Intent on how deep he intended to drive the object into her, she was slow to comprehend he'd closed his fingers over the clamp imprisoning her right nipple. She could only stand helpless and sweating as he drew the nipple toward him and closed his teeth over it. He nibbled. The invasion to her cunt spun one direction and then the other, rocking from side to side at the same time. She became his puppet, a helpless, silently sobbing, about to climax prisoner. She couldn't move and yet she did. Her cunt clenched, spasmed. Under the gag, she screamed.

"Sara! Sara!" Leaning close to her ear, Mace repeated her name over and over again. Afraid her wild thrashing would cause her to injure herself, he held her against the bed. She wouldn't want Esta and Jerome to hear so he kept his hand over her mouth. "You're having a nightmare, a nightmare." He spoke in a singsong tone, hoping to calm her. "You're safe. He can't touch you, do you understand? He can't get to you. I'm here."

The moon was a little over half full but positioned so its light came in her window. She opened her eyes but continued to fight him.

"It's me, Mace." He kept up the chanting tone. "I tried to go to bed, but I kept thinking about you, worrying. I decided to come see how you were—to convince myself you were all right."

She was trying to speak so he took a chance at taking her hand off her mouth. "Mace?" she whispered. "You, not…"

"No, I'm not Ronnie." He wrapped his arms around her and pulled her into a sitting position, then pressed her against his chest. She sank into him, shuddering and crying at the same time.

Damn it, he'd let the nightmare go on too long. He should have pulled her out of it before this, but he'd needed to see how the dream would play out—to convince himself that damnable dead Ronnie couldn't do any more than invade her sleep. But the way she'd acted, he wasn't sure.

"It was a nightmare," he said. He wasn't sure either of them believed that. "Pretty vivid but nothing more."

She straightened. "No," she said. "You're wrong."

Don't ask for an explanation. You don't want to go there — and neither does she. "Tell me," he said. He started to take hold of her wrists, but she winced and pulled free. "What's wrong?" he asked.

"They hurt."

More than her wrists had abrasions on them, he realized once he'd turned on the light. Around her neck was what looked like a rope burn. She tried to hold the sheet over her breasts, but he pulled it away, then wished to hell he hadn't. Red, painful looking indentions bracketed both nipples. She showed him another rope burn around her right ankle but kept her legs together. He didn't push.

"Where's your first aid supplies?" he asked. He didn't recognize the calm voice asking the question.

When she said they were in the bathroom, he asked if she'd be all right long enough for him to get something. She assured him she was fine. Just the same, he rushed about grabbing everything he thought she might need.

She was sitting on the side of the bed when he returned, her fingers clenching the sheet on her lap.

"Tell me," he said as he began cleaning her neck. "Everything."

"I…don't want to."

"You have to. Our lives are at stake."

That must have gotten to her because as he tended to her neck, wrists, and ankle, she took him step-by-step through the most vivid dream he'd ever heard. Only it hadn't been a dream. He'd seen the proof that Ronnie Parmenter had sexually abused his wife. At one point in her telling, the grandfather clock in the living room gonged 1 a.m. Fortunately her wounds—at least the ones he could see—were superficial. Finally, she finished. He gazed into her haunted eyes.

"I need to see your sexual organs, Sara. The way you're acting, I know they hurt."

"I-I don't want to be touched there."

"I understand." *Was this really happening, was it?* "But you can't see yourself down there, and if there's been damage…"

"Do it," she whispered and lay back down. "Just do it."

He'd never felt more tender toward a woman—not even his emotionally wounded sister—as he gently separated her legs and positioned the lamp so he had a clear view of her vaginal area. To his relief, he saw no abrasions or wounds, only red and swollen flesh. He used soap and a washcloth to clean and wipe away her body's juices. Then although beyond all reason he wanted to kiss her pussy, he applied salve to her lips, clitoral hood, and the entrance to her vagina. He suspected she didn't want her clit administered to so only placed salve around it. When she closed her legs again, enough lotion would be transferred to her most responsive organ.

"It's all right." He helped her sit up. "He didn't—he didn't hurt you."

"Didn't he?" She looked, not at him, but at the moon. "Mace, he's going to kill me."

"No he isn't. I won't let him get to you." *Somehow I'll keep the monster away!*

Chapter Thirteen

☙

The second pregnant mare gave birth to a colt in the morning, which gave Sara something wonderful to think about. Then as she and Esta were cleaning up the kitchen after a late breakfast, the realtor arrived. She'd been afraid he'd tell them they'd have to put a low price on the ranch in order to sell it, but he sounded optimistic.

"Get some of those repairs done, especially the stairs and roof. And you're right about removing as much clutter as possible." The realtor directed his comments at Mace who'd made himself part of the discussion. "But don't kill yourself. You wouldn't believe how many wealthy people want a back-to-nature experience. There's not that much open space left. Those with money are determined to snatch it up."

"You heard what he said," Mace told her once the realtor had left with the agreement giving him the listing. "The trailer has to go. No delays getting rid of it this time, either."

She took a less than steady breath. "What if *he* won't let me?"

"He'll have to go through me."

How she wanted to believe him, but her dead husband terrified her. If Ronnie did anything to Mace —

If Ronnie threatened Mace, she'd make Mace leave. His life depended on it.

You should walk out of his life now, some part of her warned. *Ronnie is the devil. No one is safe around him.*

Instead, Sara spent the rest of the day on the roof with Mace. Although she struggled to match his pace, last night's nightmare took its toll. By the time they descended the ladder for the last time, she was filthy and exhausted, hardly a vision of womanhood.

"I want to have sex with you," Mace told her as she came out of the bathroom after a shower. "But you need time to recover from the last time."

He'd dropped everything except his briefs in the laundry and stood in front of her nearly naked and beautiful. Despite everything Ronnie had done to her last night, she wanted to open her legs and give herself to the man who was keeping her sane.

Mace ran his knuckles along the side of her neck. "I'm not going to touch you beyond this," he said. "Because if I do, we both know how it'll turn out. I want you to crawl into bed alone, but I'll be nearby. Protecting you."

Mace's promise got her through the evening, and she fell asleep as soon as her head hit the pillow. She woke up once to go to the bathroom and spotted him sprawled on the chair in the little room, snoring lightly. Careful to keep her thoughts in hibernation, she again slid under the covers.

* * * * *

A tow truck was due in the afternoon to haul the trailer away. Mace hadn't known how Esta and Jerome would react to his plans for what had been their *son's* home, but neither objected.

"They were dismayed when Ronnie said the two of us would be living in it," Sara explained as they looked at the metal hunk. "They wanted us to have better for our honeymoon cottage." She laughed bitterly. "But when Ronnie told them he'd do what he damn well pleased, they didn't say anything else."

"He cursed them?"

"That's the way he always talked." She'd put on a tool belt in preparation for another day of nailing shingles and kept running her fingers over the roofing hammer. "They were used to it."

He wanted to insist that was no excuse, but if he did, he risked distracting himself from what he had to say. When she started up the ladder, he took hold of her ankle.

"Sara, he needs to know you aren't afraid of him."

She didn't look down at him. "I wish it was that easy."

"So do I."

After descending, she leaned against the ladder and wrapped her arms around her middle. "Once he died, I felt free—except for the nightmares." She shuddered and stroked her faintly bruised wrists. "But it's become more than a nightmare. He's here. So strong."

Because I brought his strength with me. His strength and fury. "Sara, you need to be gone when the trailer is hauled away. I don't want that bastard believing you had anything to do with what's going to happen to it."

Fear all but oozed from her; she went pale. "No," she whispered. "Mace, I spent too long cowering before him." She held out his hand and of course he took it. "From the first time he hit me, I didn't...I didn't know what to do."

"I'm so sorry." He pulled her close.

Although the way she clung to him left no doubt of her vulnerability, she shook her head. "It was my fault. I thought, oh God, I honestly believed he loved me because he kept saying he'd never let me go. Stupid, stupid, stupid."

"He overwhelmed you. Don't blame yourself for—"

"Then whose fault is it?" she insisted and jerked free. "I'm a grown woman, reasonably intelligent. Even when my life was at risk, I tried to hide from him instead of having him arrested."

He suspected her silence had to do with her love for Esta and Jerome. "You started divorce proceedings. You got a restraining order."

"Yes." She gave him a wry smile. "Not that it changed

him. Damn. Damn!" She pressed her hand against her forehead. "I don't usually curse. But I am so damn tired of being afraid. The last nightmare—being helpless—I don't ever want to feel like that again."

She straightened, and color returned to her cheeks. The marks around her neck seemed to fade. "No." Her tone was firm. "I refuse to hide any more."

* * * * *

Despite her bold words, when the large truck began pulling the trailer away, Sara felt sick to her stomach. She couldn't imagine ever telling Mace about the time Ronnie had wrapped duct tape around her from head to toes and left her on the living room floor while he drank himself into oblivion. In the morning, he'd undone her hips and legs, laughing because tearing off the tape had taken hair with it. He'd allowed her to use the bathroom, then ordered her to sit on the edge of the couch with her legs spread. He'd used more duct tape to secure her ankles to the couch legs and had spent the morning fucking her with his cock, empty beer bottles, even the broom handle. By the time he'd finished, she felt too humiliated to do more than crawl into the shower.

Then there'd been the time he'd brought home a portable dog kennel and shoved her naked into it before going off for the night. Even if he hadn't put in the sound deadening boards, she wouldn't have called for help and risked Jerome and Esta seeing her looking like a whipped pet.

No more! Crouching on the side of the roof, she clutched the hammer and stared down at the trailer until she could no longer see it. *No more!*

"How do you feel?" Mace asked. He'd helped the tow truck driver get the trailer ready to move while she'd remained on the roof, but now he'd rejoined her.

"Good." Surprisingly, she did. "As if I've ended a chapter in my life."

"I hope you have," he said. "I hope we both have," he added in a low tone. He indicated her hammer. "Are you fantasizing about using it on him?"

"It's a wonderful thought." The spot where the trailer had resided looked both deserted and lost as if unsure of its next role. "I think—if I'd believed I could get away with it, I would have killed him. Maybe that makes me evil, but I'm not going to apologize."

He studied her so long she began to feel uncomfortable. Mace should know how she felt about the monster she'd once been married to, but he hadn't seen what Ronnie had been capable of. He knew nothing except what she'd told him.

"You're spending the night with me," Mace said. "In the barn."

"Esta and Jerome—"

"They know something's happening between us. Besides—" He touched the side of her neck. "I'm not leaving you alone."

Chapter Fourteen

ജ

Sara hung over the top of the box stall watching the youngest foal nurse. She and Mace had entered the barn together, but he'd gone to the far end for something for the mares to eat. Although she felt a bit like a bride on her wedding night, she allowed the sight of new life to distract her.

"He's going to be a beauty," Mace said as he threw hay over the railing. "Look at those legs. He's built for speed."

"Yes, he is." She inhaled the rich scent of hay. "I don't think we're going to have much trouble selling both mares and their foals. The key is to let girls see them. I've never known a girl who wasn't crazy about baby horses."

Mace closed his arm around her waist. "You included?"

"Of course. My father was never around, and my mother spent most of her money on beer, but I used to go over to the neighbor's and clean out his stall in exchange for getting to ride."

His grip tightened. "I know so little about you."

"No less than I know about you," she told him although in truth she wasn't interested in anything except the promise and danger of his caress.

"We're going to have to do something about that, Sara." His hand slipped between her legs. "In fact…"

"In fact what?"

"Nothing." He pressed his thumb against her pussy, making an impact despite her jeans' barrier. "We'll talk about it later."

Her hands shook as she reached for the fastening on her

jeans. If there'd been more than low wattage lights over each stall, she might have had an easier time believing the night was for her and Mace alone. Maybe.

Determined not to let apprehension have the upper hand, she finished the unhooking and turned toward Mace. Shadows laced his features, but his darkness was nothing like Ronnie's had been.

Leave me, Ronnie. You'll never own me again.

"You're thinking about him." Mace stood with his thumbs hooked over his waistband.

"No." She shook her head so hard she made herself dizzy. "No, I'm not."

"Then what?"

Sexual need rushed over her; she went with the emotion. "About you. Spending the night with you."

"No reservations?" He tugged her shirttail free.

"None. I'm alive, Mace. A woman. I want sex. I need it."

He watched her fumble with her buttons, and if he was amused because she couldn't keep her fingers steady, he gave no indication. The last time they'd been together, he'd remained fully dressed, safe while she'd stood naked before him. He'd turned her body into something magical. Oh, how she wanted that again!

"This feels right," she told him. "Everything you and I have been before this night and everything that's going to happen in the future doesn't matter. Only now does."

"Only now," he repeated after a too-long silence. He clenched his jaw and shook his head before drawing the shirt off her shoulders. He slid it down her back a few inches, gripped the end, and pulled her close. She felt, not trapped, but cherished.

He tugged until her pelvis found him. Leaning back, she concentrated on the feel of his erect cock on her belly. She hoped he'd kiss her, but he tied a knot in the shirt hem. When he'd satisfied himself that she'd have to work at getting out of the makeshift straightjacket, he turned her away from him and unfastened her bra. Next he slid the straps off her shoulder and exposed her breasts but left the garment bunched around her shirt.

"How do you feel about being my prisoner?" he asked.

"Prisoner?" She lifted her arms to demonstrate how easily she could free herself. "In your dreams."

"No, not my dreams." Leaning down, he ran his tongue over each nipple. "Yours. If you can handle a little play bondage that is."

Play was good—with this man. "What did you have in mind?"

"That's right," he growled. He closed his teeth over her right nipple and drew back a little, stretching out her nipple. Then he released it. "Make me do all the work."

Do that again, please! "I think...I think you're doing a great job."

"Ah, a compliment." He did the same with her left breast before backing her against the corral fencing. Once he had her where he wanted her, he knelt and removed her shoes and socks, Next he dragged her jeans and underpants down until they bunched around her thighs.

"Now there's a sight for a horny man. A woman all done up in bows for him."

"Bows?" She looked down at herself, then giggled. "I look more like a calf trussed for branding."

"Not a chance." He stroked her belly, causing her breath to catch. "I'd never harm that beautiful flesh."

Call me beautiful. I need it.

Before she could decide whether to admit that, he picked her up and threw her over his shoulder. Giggling, she balanced herself as best she could, grateful for his securing grip around her hips. Giving into the fantasy, she let her head hang. She was Mace's prisoner, his sex toy to do with what he wanted. Just like that she'd become his possession, his slave. But because he was a kind and considerate master —

The thought, along with her breath, was knocked from her as he dropped her on her back on the bed. The old mattress absorbed her weight. She looked up at him.

"Ah." He twirled an imaginary mustache. "Spoils of the war. Now, what am I going to do with my conquest?" He pretended to debate the question while she fought need. He started to sit beside her, a simple act that caused juice to slide from her pussy. "What's that?" He pointed between her legs. "The prisoner isn't as intimidated as she'd like the conquering lord to believe."

"No, master, I am not."

"Hmm. Just don't tell my men. Otherwise, they'll stop calling me the scourge of — where are we anyway?"

"The back of nowhere," she admitted on a giggle that did nothing to quiet the wonderful excitement she felt. This was fun! Fun!

"Oh yes. A place so remote it isn't on the maps. Not much of a conqueror am I if that's all I've accomplished." Winking, he ran a thumb between her legs near her cunt. She felt him gather up some of the juice she'd provided. "Methinks the lady wants the same thing her lord does."

I do, she told him with her eyes. *I do.*

He must have understood because he stripped off his clothes, then tugged at her jeans and panties, and deposited them on top of his. Next he untied her shirt and yanked it out from under her. She started to open her legs.

"No." He pressed down on her thighs. "Not that way, Sara." He perched on the bed, then leaned low to run his tongue into her pubic hair. The simple touch nearly caused her to come. He increased the pressure on her thighs, preventing her from lifting her pussy toward him.

"I want to try something, Sara. I have some idea how

107

your husband treated you. I want to see if we can get past that."

She placed her hands over his wrists and waited, watched.

"He got off on making you feel less than human, didn't he?"

Fighting tears, she nodded. Couldn't they just fuck each other?

"We're going to go there."

Every word felt like a blow. A heartbeat later, she replayed his tone of voice and heard his gentleness. "What do you mean?" she asked.

"Some more role-playing. For tonight, I think that'll be enough. Maybe we won't have to go there again, but if we do, at least you'll understand."

This was too complex for her to think about. She forced herself to relax her grip on his wrists. He kissed her tenderly between her breasts and trailed his damp tongue over her flesh. Then, the movement strong and smooth, he rolled her over onto her stomach and bent her knees so her ass was in the air, her forehead against the bed and her arms out to the side. Old unwanted memories lapped at her sanity.

"You can't see me," he whispered. "You don't know when I'm going to touch you or in what way. All you can do is wait and believe I'll be gentle."

This isn't Ronnie's voice.

"You're waiting, waiting." He pressed his thumb against the back of her neck and began a slow, electric march down her spinal column. "Wondering what's going to happen next. You've turned your body over to me. It's mine to do what I want to with." Pressure built around her tailbone. Deeper and deeper it went until the pushing sensation transferred to her pussy. Despite her near immobility, she managed to thrust her ass toward him.

She all but purred when he spread both hands over her

ass and pulled her buttocks apart. They hadn't bothered with the lamp, which meant he had no clear view of her crack or anus. That served as little comfort when he placed one hand in her crack. Her buttocks tightened.

"It's a question of who is holding the upper hand," he told her. "Yes, technically speaking I'm on top. But you've trapped me."

"I-I don't feel in charge." *In heat, yes.*

"I don't want you to." He kept his hand against her anus and reached around with the other to cradle a dangling breast. "I don't know if surrender will ever come easy to you, but there's a huge difference between what's happening now—" He flattened her breast against her chest wall. "And what your husband did to you, isn't there?"

"Yes." Her voice sounded muffled.

To her discomfort and delight, he worked his hand from her butt hole around to her labia. His touch felt like feathers— a delicious tickling that made her sob in anticipation.

"What's this?" He dipped a finger into her vagina, electrified her with a circular motion. "Fresh wet?"

"Yes!" *Wet, no. Flood, yes.*

"This is called doggy style." His tone turned serious. "You know that, don't you?"

"Yes." She drew her arms under her and lifted her head off the bed but didn't move beyond that. She also didn't look back at the man who held her from cunt to breast. She indeed looked like a dog with all four legs on the ground—a bitch in heat presenting her sex.

"Depending on how it's done and how the people involved think about it, this can be degrading or erotic." Pulling out of her, he started rubbing the heel of his hand over the length of her sex.

Her face felt on fire. Arching her back, she struggled to move at counterpoint to him to increase the feel of having her cunt massaged. Because she was so slick there, his palm glided effortlessly over her. She felt her thigh muscles tighten, lowered her head, and shoved her ass at him again.

"She wants it?"

'Sh-she needs it!"

His stroke lengthened, and he caressed her belly button, stomach, mons, pussy, anus, all the way up and over her buttocks. Melting! On fire! Both at the same time!

"Not yet, Sara." Mace's voice seemed more growl than spoken word. "And not like this."

Before she could begin to comprehend what he had in mind, he pulled her up and onto his lap with her back against his chest. Needing to feel him everywhere, she leaned toward him and scooted closer. She found herself staring down at his cock jutting up from between her legs. She took it in her hot and sweaty hand, then lifted herself, and guided it into her.

"My turn, my turn," she chanted. She started moving up and down, her fingers spread over his thigh to keep her balance. He clenched a hand around her waist and thrust repeatedly up and into her.

She felt his quick, hot breaths on her back and reached down to gently squeeze his balls.

She found his timing, his rhythm. Her breasts became hot. Her pussy caught fire, wet and heat combining and then radiating out. Some small part of her fought the tumbling loss of self-control, but the voice was too faint to heed. Instead, she became her cunt, diving into the powerful sensations. Mace's cock pushed deep, slid out a little, rammed yet deeper. Back arched, still gripping his thigh and balls, she lost touch with everything else.

She heard, faintly, his grunts. Her own growls grew louder and more insistent. Wrapped in night with her sex partner in and over and under her, she ordered her muscles to strain. She could ride his cock like this forever, splinter until there was nothing left of her.

Shattered. Growling like a wild beast.

Chapter Fifteen

ဆ

Ball gag.

Sara stiffened but didn't move when Ronnie came at her. Instead, she fought for control, the struggle lasting until he grabbed her hair and yanked her head back. Then terror overrode everything, and she bolted.

Her flight lasted less than a step because ankle chains stopped her. Sobbing, she fell face first onto the dirt. He hadn't chained her hands, and she used them to wrestle herself onto her right hip. Ronnie stood over her, the gag dangling from his fingers.

"Naked bitch," he bit out, unnecessarily reminding her of her vulnerability. He wanted her to beg and fight the chains that held her legs together, but she wouldn't, couldn't give him that part of herself.

"You knew I was coming home." He kicked her arms out from under her and sent her sprawling to the dusty earth. "I told you I wanted my wife waiting for me, waiting and ready to be fucked, but you defied me, bitch."

What could she say, that he'd lied and said he'd be gone another week, thus giving her time to collect the money she'd made selling garden produce and use it to flee?

"I knew what you had in mind." He captured a forearm and started dragging her toward a level area. Without the use of her legs, she had little way of resisting. He hauled her over something that dug into her hip and forced out a cry. He stopped, then flipped her over onto her belly as if she weighed no more than a kitten. "Knew you were going to try to leave."

He knelt with his knees on her back and pulled up and back on the arm he still held. She felt metal close around her wrist. Terror burned. She tried to pull her arm free. He laughed and pressed yet more weight into her back. She couldn't breathe!

"No more fight left in you, bitch." He grabbed her other arm and forced it back so he could handcuff her wrists together. "Don't know whether I should be mad because you tried to run or thank you for providing entertainment."

He slid off her and rolled her onto her side. He made a show of letting her see the ball gag. "I know how you are when you get off, loud enough to wake the dead." He grabbed her hair and pulled back, then shoved the ball between her teeth. Releasing her hair, he pushed her face into the ground and fastened the leather straps behind her head. Sitting cross-legged beside her, he waited for her to lift her head. Then he patted her cheek. "There, isn't that better? Now you can scream to your heart's content and not worry about waking the neighbors."

When he got to his feet and walked out of sight, she lay in the dust and waited, straining to hear. He returned, holding a small bag he'd been carrying when he walked in the door earlier. A profound sense of weakness assaulted her as she recalled the chains and gag he'd pulled out of it.

"Kind of nice out here, isn't it?" Making his point, he picked up some dust and sprinkled it over her breasts. "This is just how a loving couple should spend their time together – getting reacquainted in the wilderness."

When he'd spotted her suitcase on the bed, he'd thrown her in the trunk of his car and driven her out here. By then she'd been half-unconscious from lack of oxygen and hadn't put up a fight as he ripped off her clothes. She'd tried to fight off the ankle restraints, but the trunk had been too confining. Then he'd hefted her out and forced her to take mincing steps until she could no longer see the car. That's when he'd showed her the disgusting gag.

He pulled several lengths of white rope out of the bag and dragged them over her breasts and belly. He tried to get them to slide between her legs, but the ankle restraints made that impossible. "Well, shit. Fortunately – " He forced his hand against her cunt and pushed upward. "Fortunately, there's more than one way to skin a cat." After poking and prodding in a futile attempt to get his fingers in her vagina, he turned his attention back to the ropes.

"You belong to me, Sara. I'd think you'd remember."

112

When he placed her on her stomach again, she knew better than to fight. He was doing something with her handcuffs, but she couldn't tell what until he let go of the restraints, and her hands rested against her ass. Along with the hard metal on her buttocks, she now felt a loose length of rope.

"That got your attention?" He ran the end of the rope between her ass cheeks. "Eager to see what new toy I've got for us to play with, are you?" He patted her ass almost lovingly. "Of course you are, my sweet. Poor woman, left alone for too long – nothing to do except think about how your man's going to fuck your brains out when he gets home. Well, he's home. The game begins."

He grabbed the chain between her ankles and pulled her legs up and back so her heels ground into her buttocks. When he looped the rope over the ankle chain and pulled tight, she understood. She'd been hogtied – arms and legs locked together, her body motionless.

"Maybe a game isn't the right word." He shoved her onto her side so she could see him again. "Because I'm the only one who knows what the rules are."

Survival depended on staying on top of panic, but when he sat beside her so he could stroke a breast, self-control became fragile. The man she'd married back in her lonely ignorance was capable of unbelievable cruelty. He knew she'd been going to leave him. If he decided to make her pay the ultimate price –

To her surprise, he only continued to stroke her breast. "You're beautiful, Sara," he muttered. "The most beautiful woman I've ever known." He ran a finger under the strap that kept the ball in her mouth. "When you said you'd marry me, I considered myself the luckiest man on earth. I wanted to give you everything – have you love me as much as I love you."

Her muscles felt loose. Was she floating?

"I've never known how to show you how I feel. You deserve a mansion, but all I could give you was that shit hole of a trailer." Shifting position, he began caressing her throat. Although experience had shown her how cruel he could be, she lived in the moment. Her husband, the man she'd vowed to love and honor, was treating her like something precious – except for the ropes and chains.

"I figured I'd never get married," he continued. "That no woman would want me. Then…" His hands on her throat and breast stilled. "Why did it change, Sara? When did you stop loving me?"

When you started hurting and scaring me, she wanted to say, but of course he'd rendered her speechless.

"You bring out my dark side." His fingers stretched over her throat. He began applying pressure. "It's always been there. I don't know how to stop it. The world starts feeling out of control. I become an animal caught in a flood, fighting with everything in me to get somewhere safe, but I know it isn't going to happen." He clamped down around her throat, cutting off her breath. Then he slid away and clenched his hands. His eyes burned with an awful fury.

"Around you I'm in control. The man." Rocking forward, he grabbed her shoulders and hips and wrenched her onto her back so her bound arms and legs bore her weight. "Don't you understand?" He sprang to his feet and straddled her, leaning over so she felt him everywhere and he became her world. "You're the only living thing I own. I can't let you leave – I won't!"

With that, he again dropped beside her and forced her knees apart. Because she'd arched her back to take some of the pressure off her legs, she could barely see him.

"There it is," he announced as he pressed the heel of his hand against her pussy. "The mother lode." He rocked his heel back and forth, creating hot, unwanted friction throughout her sex. "You're not going to leave me, Sara. How can you even think it when I'm the only man who knows how to turn you on?"

The strain in her shoulders and thighs should have been enough to distract her from his manipulations, but much as she hated admitting it, he was right. Her cunt was a primitive organ. It cared nothing about what went on in her mind.

"This is our playground, Sara." Switching his attack, he ran his forefinger from her mons to her clit. He pressed, released, stroked. With every touch her self-control splintered a bit more. She moaned under the gag. No matter how hard she tried not to, her head began rocking from side to side. She couldn't tell whether he was still keeping her knees apart, couldn't muster the will to try to close herself to him.

"*This is your switch, Sara. And because I know how to make you hungry, I'll never have to force myself on you.*" *He caught her hot and swollen clit and pulled. Her head roared; she started to catch fire.*

Then from somewhere deep inside, something shifted. A small, sane part of her mind understood that what was happening in the dirt had nothing to do with a man's love or even regard for his wife. Ronnie might have once been a lonely and unloved boy, but he was no longer that innocent child. He'd become an adult who dealt with his failures via chains, ropes, sexual manipulation.

Even as her cunt continued to respond as nature had intended, she divorced herself from it, shut it off, refused to acknowledge its existence. The fire in her veins cooled. Her head stopped throbbing. She tasted the hard rubber in her mouth, felt dirt in her hair and on her skin, smelled not just her own loathing-laced sweat but Ronnie's as well.

His manipulation of her cunt became more insistent, but it didn't matter. He couldn't hurt her because — why?

"*Damn it! Damn it! What the hell?*"

Feeling removed from her surroundings, her bonds, but most of all from the man who loved to terrify and torment her, she focused on him. She couldn't speak because this was his way of turning her into something inhuman, but she didn't need to. Her unresponsive body and hard, direct gaze said it all.

No matter what you do to me, she told him in all the ways that mattered, you can't destroy my will.

Defeat flickered over his features. Then he turned his hands into weapons and began hammering her sides.

* * * * *

Mace had been lying beside Sara since she started moaning. Her body had contorted as if she'd been hogtied, but much as he wanted to take her from her nightmare, he didn't. Not only did he need to know whether she could free herself on her own, he had to learn as much as possible about Ronnie's impact.

115

Then she'd started violently recoiling and sobbing as if she was being strangled, and he couldn't take it any more.

"Sara, Sara!" Although she fought him, he held her. He kept repeating her name, and in his mind, he began attacking whoever had been hurting her. *Whoever? As if he didn't know.*

"Sara, honey, it's all right," he crooned. Her contortions let up, and she was no longer twisted in that impossible position. She opened her eyes, and he kissed her repeatedly. "You had a nightmare," he said when he was done. He still cradled her body against his.

"No," she muttered. "Not a nightmare."

"Damn him! What did he do? Tell me, what did he do?"

She shuddered but didn't cry. "You don't want to know," she whispered before wrapping her arms around him.

"Yes," he made himself say, "I do." He tried to help her into a sitting position, then stopped when she cried out.

"What is it?" he asked.

"My side. He hit—he started hitting—"

"Damn you!" Willing the damnable coward to face his fury, Mace stared into the darkness. He sensed something. "You're dead, you bastard. You belong in hell. Go back there! Leave her alone!"

"He won't," Sara said. Although he could tell it caused her pain, she kissed him and ran her hands over his neck. "H-he isn't done with me."

With us.

Chapter Sixteen

ଌ

Neither of them had fallen back to sleep. Much as Mace had wanted to offer Sara forgetfulness via the act of sex, she hadn't been in any shape for it. He'd been afraid Ronnie had broken her ribs, but after gently examining her, he'd assured himself that the abuse hadn't gone that far. She hadn't wanted to talk about what had taken place, but between what little she'd said and what he'd observed, he had a pretty good idea.

As morning came, he managed to corral enough of his fury at Ronnie to note the clear, clean sky, but he couldn't do anything about the weight on his heart.

He shouldn't have come here! And even if that decision had been taken out of his hands by his reaction to the photograph, he certainly shouldn't have stayed. His presence had awakened something in a monster that should be dead. If he hadn't infringed on Sara's life, she'd be safe.

Or would she?

The question pounded at him. No matter how much he fought to silence it, it refused to go away, and in the end, he acknowledged the truth. Walking into Sara's world, especially fucking her, had pushed Ronnie in new and dangerous ways, but the beast existed in a form and way that defied explanation and control.

Ronnie wanted Sara to himself, to torment and torture. Today, tomorrow, five years from now wouldn't make a difference. Sooner or later he'd lose control and kill her.

"And you're the one to stop him, you know you are," he muttered as he led the two mares and their newborns outside.

He'd wondered whether Esta and Jerome would notice

the way Sara favored her side, but the realtor had called as the elderly couple was getting up. He had a client who was interested in the property. Could he bring them by in the afternoon?

"I'm not getting my hopes up," Jerome said. Just the same, he asked his wife if he should wear one of his goin'-to-town shirts.

Esta began bustling about straightening the living room and stewing that the rickety front steps would turn off any potential buyer.

"If you want, I'll take care of that instead of finishing the roofing today," Mace offered. "Besides—" He gave Sara a sideways look. "I think she needs to rest."

"Oh?" Esta looked confused. "Oh, my dear." She reached out to hug Sara. Fortunately, Sara managed to evade what would have been a hard embrace. "Of course," Esta continued. "You shouldn't be crawling around on the roof like that."

"I'm fine."

"That's what you always say." Esta turned toward Mace. "I used to think she was accident-prone the way she was always bruising herself. At least she's learned to take better care of herself. Why, I can't remember the last time you got hurt."

No one said anything, but soon after, Jerome said he wanted to consult with Mace about the best way to repair the steps.

"They weren't no damn accidents," Jerome said once they were outside. "I don't know why my wife won't admit it. She wanted children so bad; I guess that's what blinded her to what that boy was capable of."

"Did you talk to Sara about it?" Mace asked.

"You damn bet I did. And I told her I'd give her the money to get away. At first she wouldn't talk to me about what was going on—her old man had never been around, and I don't think she knew how to act around me, whether she could trust anyone—but then she asked if the offer still held. Of course I gave money to her right off, but the way things turned out, she didn't need it."

Because Ronnie was killed. Because I —

"Jerome, can I ask you something?"

Jerome just looked at him.

"Were you ever afraid of Ronnie?"

"Yeah," the older man admitted, "I was. But he never laid a hand on the woman he called Mother. I told myself at least he had some goodness in him."

Not enough.

* * * * *

Sara hadn't given much thought to what would happen when the realtor showed up. In truth, she couldn't stop thinking about last night. Now, as she watched the couple she guessed were in their late 40's explore the ranch, she found herself wondering what it would feel like to be comfortable around one's spouse. Esta and Jerome had that same easy way, as if they were halves of a whole. It had never been like that between her and Ronnie.

Instead, her husband had tried to break her spirit. If she'd put an end to his cruelty at the beginning, maybe he wouldn't still be here—forcing her back in time instead of letting her embrace the future.

Embrace Mace.

It had only taken Mace a couple of hours to replace the front steps. At the moment he was straddling the roof as he secured the ridge cap in place. She could only imagine the tension in his leg muscles as he held himself in place.

Any other man would have run from a woman haunted by her dead husband. Instead, he'd taken her to his bed and body. More than that, he'd let her know he'd listen to her nightmares.

But if you know everything that happened in that horrible trailer and in the dirt — and other places — would it repulse you? Would you turn your back on me?

There was only one way to find out.

* * * * *

"Who knows what's going to happen, but right now I have a good feeling about it."

"So do I," Sara admitted. "They were here so long and asked so many questions — questions that showed they're no strangers to ranching — wouldn't it be something if the place sells right away?"

She and Mace were sitting on the front porch sipping iced tea and watching the sun set. Esta and Jerome had just taken off for a square dance at the grange ten miles down the road. When the older couple had announced their plans for the evening, she hadn't known whether to be uneasy or grateful because she and Mace would have some time together.

As he turned toward her, she acknowledged she felt a bit of both. "Mace?" She swallowed and tried again. "I've made a decision."

"What?"

Placing her tea on the small table between them, she faced him. "The company that took the trailer — I want them to do the same thing to Ronnie's car."

"Why?" Mace finally said.

"The memories." *Don't! For once in your life, don't hide!* "Mace, the only way I'm going to be free of him is by getting rid of everything I associate with him. If he sees I want nothing to do with him —"

"He's dead."

"No, he isn't!" She sprang to her feet and stalked to the porch railing, then forced herself to face him. "You know he isn't."

"Yes. I do."

He leaned forward but made no move to touch her. "I think—hell, I don't know what I think. Everything that's happened since Ronnie walked into my life—none of it makes sense." *Stop sounding like an idiot.* "Last night wasn't a nightmare," she said softly. "I was reliving something that happened between Ronnie and me. Something he did to me."

"Yes."

Yes, as in you already knew? "Even now—" She glanced at the encroaching night. "I feel his weight, his temper. But I'm not going to cower any more! I'm not!"

Mace stood and joined her at the railing. "The car?" he prompted.

"The car," she repeated and closed her eyes. To her relief, awareness of Mace's body became stronger than her fear. "Mace, things happened between Ronnie and me in the trailer—it was his kingdom. I became his—his slave." She'd never needed anything more than she needed Mace holding her, but if she gave in, she might not finish what he needed to know.

"His anger at the world, his hatred of himself—he took it out on me in that place. You saw the sound-deadening boards—that made it possible for him to…"

"Go on."

You understand. You know I need to do this.

"His need to master and possess me happened other places too, but the trailer was *his*. He saw me in the same light."

"And the car?" Mace asked and took her hand.

"The car was power and control."

"Control of you?"

"Yes," she whispered. Night was coming so fast. Already the high desert air was turning chilly. "He, ah—Mace, if you can't handle hearing this—"

Vonna Harper

"Yeah, I can. But first we're going inside."

She let him lead the way into the house. When he indicated she should sit on the couch, she felt swamped by memories of what Ronnie had done to her there once when his parents were gone, but this telling was about the car—only the car.

"So Ronnie was into bondage," Mace said as he sat next to her and placed his hand on her knee. "And you weren't. Go on."

Go on.

Her voice shook. "The first time I saw that vehicle was after he'd bought it during one of his trips. He drove up to the trailer and yelled at me to come see it. We hadn't been married long, not long enough for me to know everything about him. I, ah, I got mad. Told him we couldn't afford it. I, ah, I went back inside."

"He came after you?"

"Yes." She again closed her eyes to better call up the unwanted but necessary memories. "He hit me in the back and knocked me to the floor. I'd had the breath knocked out of me and didn't fight while he ripped off my jeans. Then—then he removed his belt. I thought he was going to beat me so I tried to crawl away."

In her mind, she saw herself half-naked and terrified scrambling on hands and knees, her ass presented to Ronnie as she made a desperate try to reach—reach what?

"He stuck me once on the buttocks." *Keep your eyes closed. That way you don't have to see the look on Mace's face.* "Then he straddled me and sat on me, flattened me under him."

Mace muttered a curse. He stroked her knee.

"Then…then he used the belt to tie my hands behind me. I was crying and begging him to stop. He always carried a pocketknife. He used that to cut off my shirt and bra. Then—" she took a shuddering breath, "he gagged me with the shirt. I was so scared I couldn't think. I, ah, I don't know what he tied

122

my feet with. He pulled me up and threw me over his shoulder. He was so strong."

"Sara?"

"What?" She still couldn't make herself open her eyes.

"You don't have to tell me everything right away."

I don't ever want you to know this. "No," she told him. "It's all right." Finally she looked at him. "Unless you don't want—"

"I don't." He kissed the tip of her nose; his smile was so gentle it nearly did her in. "But this has to be done."

And if you can't handle it, at least I'll know. "You're right. I—Ronnie needs to accept responsibility for killing what feelings I once had for him. To realize how despicable his behavior was." Saying those things helped her focus on more than the memory of being under her husband's control. "He took me outside and threw me in the back seat."

"It's a sports car. There's hardly any room."

"No, there isn't. I'd landed on my back. He hooked the lap seatbelt around my breasts and cinched it so tight I couldn't move." She dropped her gaze to Mace's hand, thinking that although his was larger than Ronnie's, his touch had always been gentle. "Then he untied my ankles and tried to force my legs apart. I fought him—until he started slapping my thighs and yelling he'd use a riding crop if I didn't let him do what he wanted."

A shudder rolled over her. Even in the cozy room with its smells of baking bread and Mace beside her, she couldn't fight the pull into the past. "He wedged my right leg between the two front bucket seats and jammed the other against the back headrest. I was so scared—I couldn't think. I was certain he was going to rape me. He tried, but he couldn't fit himself in that small space so he—so he used a flashlight. At least he did for a while. Then he pulled me toward him so my legs dangled out of the car. It—that gave him the room he needed."

"He raped you."

Despite her self-loathing, she shook her head. "He didn't enter me for a while, not until he'd played with my—my pussy and gotten me all wet. I hated it, but I couldn't help myself. It was like—like my clit didn't care about anything except being excited. At least—" She sucked in air. "That way when he finally took me, it didn't hurt. Much."

"But you didn't want it."

"No! Of course not! He took advantage—"

"Of your sexual nature. He capitalized on what's instinctual about a woman's body."

He understood. He didn't hate me. "Later, after he'd flipped me onto my stomach and taken me another way…" She couldn't finish.

"He fucked your ass?"

"Yes." Although it hadn't been the only time he'd done that to her, the memory made her sick. "When he couldn't get another erection, he tied my legs again and left me in the car the rest of the night."

"Why didn't you charge him with assault?"

Why? Hadn't she asked herself the same hard question a million times? "I was so ashamed. I-I tried to imagine telling the police and knew I couldn't do it."

"So did he. He used that against you."

She felt dirty, a whore. Forcing herself to her feet, she stumbled toward the door. She couldn't make herself reach for the knob and when Mace came after her and rested his hands on her shoulder, she nearly collapsed.

"Tomorrow," he said, "we'll get rid of the car."

Chapter Seventeen

ഇ

Feeling weightless, Sara turned around. The only light in the room came from a lamp, thus allowing her to step over the threshold leading from reality into fantasy. In her mind, Mace became a gift, a male animal who'd come to put an end to her loneliness. Neither of them had a past; the future didn't matter.

Not questioning what she was doing, she pushed him back toward the couch. Then she shoved, and he wound up sitting on it, looking up at her. She stared at him for a long time until she knew she'd never forget how he looked at this moment.

Her hands shook a little when she reached for the buttons on her shirt. She undid the first two buttons, then stopped and cupped her hand around her sex, feeling heat and moisture beneath the practical denim. Mace's gaze locked on what she was doing.

For several moments, she massaged herself, rocking from side to side to increase the friction. She still had one hand on her shirt but couldn't concentrate beyond the self-manipulation. Finally, what she was doing wasn't enough, and she put her mind to feeling skin against skin. Despite her best intentions, however, she couldn't release the snap.

When Mace reached for her, she stepped closer and didn't breathe while he unzipped her jeans. With his manipulations acting as her guidance, she managed to do the same to him. But when he made as if to stand, she pushed him against the couch again.

Distance between them was good. Distance put her in control — maybe.

Careful not to think, she stepped out of the slippers she'd been wearing. She loved the slow striptease act of removing her jeans and panties with Mace watching, his eyes saying he approved—anticipated. His cock expanded and found partial escape through the opening she'd made in his jeans.

He wanted her. Once she'd made herself ready for him, they'd have sex. They'd fuck. Her body would be her gift to him.

Light and freedom stole over her. She felt feather light and young when she'd felt old for too long. She heard music in her head that put her in mind of night animal sounds and Indian drums. Going with the lightness on her skin and in her veins, she turned her attention back to her shirt. This time she had no trouble with the buttons and drew out the act of gliding it off her shoulders before dropping it to the floor. Mace's lips parted. He closed his hand over his cock.

She'd turned him on. The knowledge filled her with joy. She stood before him wearing only her bra but didn't hurry removing it. Instead, she spread her legs and ran first one and then the other hand between them. With each stroke, she took note of her generous lubrication. Time after time she ministered to her sexual need, careful not to push herself too close to the edge. Her breasts felt swollen; they barely fit within the practical enclosure. The nubs pressing against fabric were so sensitive it hurt.

Self-stimulation, liking her body, feeling free with it. Acknowledging those things made her want to shout with joy. Instead, she slid close so her legs rubbed against Mace's. She took hold of his hands and pulled him to his feet. He wanted to touch her cunt, she wanted the same thing, but not yet. Slow. This was going to be slow.

When she had him in place with his hands at his sides, she pulled his jeans down off his hips but left them around his knees. Then, laughing, she again pushed him onto the couch.

"What are—?"

"Silence." She put her hand over his mouth. "Right now we aren't talking."

Smiling, he cupped his large, work-roughened hand over her vulva. When he increased the pressure on her sex, she pushed into him. She tried rocking from side to side as she'd done before, but she nearly lost her balance so simply presented herself to him.

Hot liquid flowed from her. His fingers and palm grew wet. When he began massaging her, she felt as if they were flowing together, becoming one. Having the side of his thumb stroke her clit was wonderful! How long before she came?

But the other time they'd been together, it had been all about her. She wanted to give him the same gift.

Sighing, she drew his hand off her cunt and placed it on her hip. Then she bracketed his legs with hers and sat on his thighs. She leaned forward and presented him with an open-mouthed kiss. At the same time, she scooted closer until his hard cock molded with her sex. She wanted him in her! Yes, she did. And from the way his cock felt, she had no doubt he wanted the same thing. Instead of giving into their mutual desire though, she covered his cock and held it still and safe between palm and pussy.

She looked down at what she'd done. Doing so put an end to their kiss, but it was worth it. She rolled his cock from side to side, her sex juices making the journey smooth and heady. He wrapped his arms around her so she no longer had to concentrate on her balance. Feeling secure, she leaned back a little before taking hold of the head of his cock and drawing it up a little.

It felt huge! Huge and lonely. A man's engorged cock belonged inside a woman—buried deep in her. Forgetting her plans to draw things out, she planted her legs under her, lifted her ass off him, and guided him effortlessly into her.

She housed him! Provided a home for him.

She remained standing on bent knees as he leaned back,

supporting himself by placing his hands behind him. From somewhere she found enough self-control not to rush things. Yes, her filled and dripping cunt throbbed with the need for release, and it would take little to make him come. But they had the house to themselves—this time for the two of them.

Drawing on her muscular legs, she moved up and down. At the same time, she clenched her pussy muscles and kept them tight around him. His cock slid inside her, sometimes nearly escaping. When that happened, he rose off the couch and came with her.

Time passed. Sweat pooled between her breasts. The damnable bra absorbed it. Much as she enjoyed the sensation of being in charge, her thigh muscles now felt the strain. With his hands no longer supporting her, her back had started to ache. Sighing in surrender, she climbed onto the couch, a knee on either side of his hips.

In the process of repositioning herself, she'd lost her cunt-hold on his cock. She was trying to recapture the sex-slick organ when she learned that having his back supported by the couch allowed him to use his hands. He spread his fingers over her hips and waited for her to direct his cock back in her. They were so close she couldn't be sure, but she thought he smiled as he pulled her against him.

Although she grunted, she had no objection to having her breasts mashed against his chest. She remained in his embrace, feeling him everywhere, comforted and safe, joined in the most intimate of ways. Every time he breathed, she moved with him. She wished she could think how to thank him for unfastening her bra. After what might have been a long time, he guided her back to an upright position. She waited until he'd slipped off her bra, then braced her hands against the back of the couch.

The movement smooth and nearly controlled, she again clenched his cock with her cunt muscles and rose up on her knees.

They found a rhythm, a beat of body against body. She'd

briefly forgotten how aroused she was while trying to find the right position. Realization slid back over her to heat skin, muscle, and bone. She looked down at this man she was riding, looked past the surface and found his depths. He was layers, endless layers—some deliberately kept from her. But his muscles and heat, most of all his hotly-housed cock said how much he handed her.

She gifted him in return. Naked, exposed, reaching greedily for that thing called climax—without a word she told him those things. A sob burst from her. Another followed so close she couldn't tell when the first ended.

She kept nothing from Mace, let him hear her go out of control, her hunger, her joy. She couldn't tell and didn't care whether the burning between her legs came just from fucking or whether her thigh muscles added their own heat.

She rose and fell, rose and fell, held onto his cock with all the strength in her pussy. Her head lulled to the side, forgotten under the force of her loud and joyous climax. Spasm after spasm rocked her. She literally saw stars. The spasms spread and melted into his climax. She didn't just scream, she bellowed, her voice echoing in the little room.

Chapter Eighteen

❦

Sara stood before the gap-toothed owner of the small wrecking yard, arms folded across her chest. She didn't look at Mace.

"I know I'm crazy," she said. "But it's my crazy and my decision."

"Lady." The man glanced at Mace, shook his head, and again leveled a stare at her. "This is one fine car." He jerked a thumb at the black beast Mace had driven into Prineville. She'd brought her Jeep so they'd have something to ride back in and because after what she'd told Mace about the things she'd endure in there, she couldn't bear to close herself inside it. "Look, I'll give you five hundred for it right now, five hundred cash," the man said. "That's a hell of a lot better than paying me to crush it."

"I'm not going to change my mind." Back when she'd been desperate to leave Ronnie that much money would have smelled like freedom. She could get several thousand for it if she put it up for sale. "There're a lot of bad memories that go with that vehicle."

"You're nuts, lady. Nuts."

"You've had your say." Mace spoke for the first time since they'd found the owner. He put his arm around her shoulder. "About her wanting to see it being crushed, it doesn't look as if you're so busy you can't accommodate her. After all, with what you're getting paid —"

"Shit, all right." Although his look said they both needed to be locked away, he motioned to a fat man wearing filthy overalls. When the man lumbered over, he told him to warm up the crusher.

Under Mace's guidance, she backed away from the hated car and watched as the fat man drove it under a tall piece of machinery with a huge metal plate at the top. The plate was attached to a thick cable. When the fat man revved up the machinery, the plate began swinging back and forth.

She didn't take her eyes off the car. It seemed to cower under the plate. *Die! And take him with you.*

She wasn't sure what she expected, certainly something more spectacular than what transpired. Instead of dropping the hammer-like plate from high overhead, the fat man maneuvered it down until it was only a few feet over the car. The plate thumped onto the roof, causing the windows to explode outward and the tires to flatten. Then the plate lifted and dropped again. This time the car roof imploded. With each pounding, the car lost more definition. Metal groaned, screamed really. Finally, what had once been her dungeon had been reduced to a flattened hunk.

Sara drew in a long and shaky breath.

"How do you feel?" Mace asked.

"Exhausted." She started to turn her back on the ruined mess, then stopped. It had to be her imagination of course, but for an instant she swore she saw mist float away from what had once been Ronnie's pride and joy.

* * * * *

"I can't believe it," Esta said for at least the fifth time since she'd hung up the phone. "To have an offer so soon —"

"We haven't heard it yet," her husband pointed out, also for the fifth time. "We don't know how serious they are."

Mace had a gut feeling the offer to buy the ranch was a legitimate one. He wished he could put his mind to what might happen once the realtor made his presentation in the morning, but he'd felt uneasy ever since he and Sara had returned from the wrecking yard. He couldn't shake his belief that destroying Ronnie's car hadn't changed anything and had felt a presence all afternoon.

Watching Sara deal with her former in-laws' emotions allowed him to tamp down some of his unease. Even more, he was again struck by how much his life had changed since seeing that damnable photograph—hell, ever since he'd learned of Ronnie Parmenter's existence.

If he could boil everything down to its essence, it came to one thing: he was on a train without brakes.

Taking advantage of their focus on the changes that might soon come, he excused himself, saying he needed to check his cell phone messages. Sara gave him a puzzled look as he headed outside, and he responded with what he hoped was a reassuring smile.

We'll have tonight, he said with his eyes. *For more of what we've gotten so good at.*

Instead of sitting on the porch, he headed into the dark. The further he went, the more solid the unseen presence felt.

"What the hell do you want, Ronnie?" he demanded. "You're such a miserable bastard that even in death you're bent on making a good woman's life hell?"

He heard nothing, not that he expected to. Just the same, now that he'd started, he couldn't let things be. "I never thought I believed in a bad seed, but I do now. You're so filled with hate; you can't see you had someone decent. She was ready to love you, you bastard. But you destroyed any chance you had. Don't you get it?"

He stopped and stared at the night as if willing the evil to show itself. "She isn't your possession. She proved that when you were alive. And nothing you do now is going to change it."

A blast of cold air slammed into him.

"So you are here," he challenged. Although his heart pounded, he wasn't afraid. "You want a fight, you bastard? Come after me, me! We both know why I want a piece of you—all the reasons."

More cold air raked his skin, then nothing. He wanted to repeat his challenge, but how the hell does a mortal fight—fight what?

"You know where I am," he finally said. "When you're ready to have it out, let me know."

* * * * *

The message from his foreman wasn't unexpected. So far Hugo's efforts to nail down an experienced crew for the harvest had been less than successful, in large part because a corporation that had recently bought up several small orchards was offering the workers more money.

"I'm getting to the bottom of the barrel," Hugo had said. "You have more connections than I do. Get your ass back here and start pulling some strings."

"I know," Mace muttered as if Hugo was standing beside him. "Hell, I shouldn't have come here in the first place."

No. It's too late for regret.

Although eventually he'd have to face what else it was too late for, Mace put off the question by listening to the rest of his messages. Only one held his attention.

"I never thought you'd be gone so long," his sister said. She sounded about five years old. "I know, I know, I need to stand on my own two feet. I can't always come running to you, but—do you have any idea when you'll be back?"

Guilt washed over him, and he punched her number. Judi had gotten into the habit of screening her calls, but because his cell was listed in her phone's memory, he figured she'd pick up if she was home.

She was.

"All right," she said in answer to his question about how she was doing. "I saw the shrink on Monday, but I think he's getting impatient with me."

"What makes you say that?" He leaned against the side of

the barn and concentrated on the stars.

"Because he wants me to talk about everything that led up to my — my breakdown. Mace, you know why I can't."

Part of the reason was because her mind had blocked out much of the night she'd nearly died. The other came as a result of her determination to protect his involvement. Feeling heartsick, for at least the hundredth time Mace pondered when, if ever, his sister would be strong enough for the truth.

"I'll be back as soon as I can," he told her. "I need to talk to your psychiatrist."

"What about?" She sounded frightened. "Mace, I don't need to go back to that hospital. I'm not near as bad as I was when—"

"I know you aren't, sweetie. Look, don't sweat what your psychiatrist might or might not want you to do. I'm paying his bill, and he needs to answer to me."

"Oh. I, ah, I think I'd like that. Maybe he'll tell you how I'm doing."

Better, thank God, better. Before he could deal with his relief, she asked what he meant by soon. "Hopefully by the end of the week," he told her. *And I don't think I'll be alone. I hope to hell I won't.*

* * * * *

"One thing about contemplating having the money to live wherever they want, they haven't noticed that the car is gone."

Mace muttered something.

"What is it?" Sara asked. "Did something come up during your calls—?"

"Nothing unexpected." He'd been changing the light bulb in the barn sleeping area while she held a flashlight. Now he faced her. "Sara, I have to go back before long."

She felt punched. "I see." She tried to keep emotion out of her voice.

134

Mace studied her, then frowned at the still unlit lamp. "I don't know what's wrong with it. The bulb's new. It should— Sara, I want you to come with me."

Leave with him. Leave this place with its memories, this place where I worked so hard to rebuild my self-esteem after Ronnie's death. "I see."

"Is that all you have to say?" He lit the candle, then took the flashlight from her and turned it off. He stood so close she felt him on her skin.

"I, ah, I knew you couldn't stay forever but to have it come up so soon—"

"What about my request?" He held out his hand, and she put hers in it.

All day she'd struggled with a weight she knew had to do with Ronnie, but now she felt as if she could fly. "I promised myself I wouldn't leave Esta and Jerome."

"They won't be here much longer." Without asking permission, he began unbuttoning her blouse. "Then what, Sara? What about you?"

Me. My life.

"You said you want to go to college." He drew the blouse off her shoulders and used the hem to draw her against him. "There are colleges near where I live. And warmer winters, and me."

You.

"You're shaking," he muttered.

Before she could get her throat to work, he'd dispensed with her bra and placed both garments on the stand next to the candle. In the pale light, his features flickered. She felt like a small flame, fragile yet constantly fed.

"Why *are* you shaking?" he asked.

"I want—" He'd pushed her away so he'd have access to her jeans' zipper. She could barely think beyond what he was doing. "I want you."

He didn't respond until he'd dispensed with the rest of her clothes. "You'll have me," he whispered. "All of me and all night."

He lifted her in his arms and deposited her belly down on the bed. She tucked her hands under her head and turned toward him. Her body felt languid, a small fire waiting for more fuel. Still fully clothed, he sat beside her and began trailing his fingers over her shoulder blade.

"We've been in a hurry before," he said. "Whenever we've had sex, there's been baggage in the way to say nothing of feeling as if we're in heat."

She wondered if she should tell him she was starting to feel that way again but put it off because his feather-like touch had moved to the back of her neck. Her mind followed his fingers, awareness tunneling down to her spinal column. She'd never had a massage, never known she could feel the tiny circular movements along her backbone clear to the tip of her toes.

Even before he began performing his magic on her buttocks, she'd amended her assessment of what a massage was capable of. With Mace in charge, most of what she experienced centered in her cunt, her pussy, the part of her that would never have enough of him.

"I've never had…" Her lips felt as if they'd been touched an electric current.

"What?" He patted her ass cheeks, then began kneading them. "A massage?"

"Hmm."

"I figured you haven't, and certainly not one like this."

His teasing promise caused her fingers to curl. She wanted to lift her head and kiss him but couldn't move. What had happened to the weightless sensation?

There it was, brought back by magical fingertips inching around her armpits to tease what of her flattened breasts he could reach. Before she could figure out what she should do to increase his access, he'd changed direction and was slowly tiptoeing down her spine. Her sex reminded her of the dancing candlelight—on fire.

In her mind she imagined him turning her over and opening her so he could fill the hot, empty cave. Then her ignited nerve endings brought her back to the small of her back, her buttocks. With no conscious decision on her part, her legs separated.

The thought of him taking advantage of her invitation caused a flood to ooze from her, but he didn't. Instead, he again expertly kneaded her ass cheeks. Just as she believed he'd gotten her so sensitive there she couldn't handle it any more, he ran his hands down the inside of her thighs.

She sighed, a strangled little sound.

"No complaints?" he asked.

"None."

"Good because…"

His breath floated over her ass crack, causing her to gasp. She sensed him coming closer, felt another warm puff of air. Shivering, she lifted her pelvis. Something was—

Belatedly it registered that he'd pulled her cheeks apart before lowering his head and touching his tongue to her tailbone. More shivering on her part. More tongue-touches on his. Although she swore the top of her head was coming off, she struggled to keep track of what he was doing. His tongue became magical, bathing her buttocks, her anus, what he could reach of her labial lips. She marveled at his ability to know just what she needed when and where.

She tried to tuck her knees under her so he could have access to everything, but he pressed down, keeping her in place.

"Don't rush it, Sara. Tonight, we aren't going to rush it."

That's easy for you to say.

Just the same, she did her best to go at his pace. He'd lit a sexual fire in her and he'd eventually have to pay the price. Thinking about jumping his bones gave her something to concentrate on. Her nails dug into the spread, and she rolled her head from side to side — the one thing she could move.

A fantasy began — one she never thought she'd have.

He'd taken her deep into an almond orchard. Dark, close growing trees heavy with branches and leaves isolated them from the world. In the distance she heard machinery working. He'd rendered her helpless, turned her into a pliant body he'd thrown over his shoulder and carried into the deep shadows.

Once at the secret spot he'd chosen for his purpose, he stood her on her feet. She could stand, just barely. She was already naked, her nipples hard, breasts swollen. He smiled and fingered what belonged to him, then lifted her arms over her head and tied her wrists to a rope hanging from a sturdy branch. Muscles beyond her control, she could only wait for his next move. Nothing approaching fear touched her.

Once he assured himself he'd securely tied her, he produced a large, ruby red vibrator and began using it on her breasts. She tried to hold back a long, low moan but failed. Smiling, he worked the toy lower, over her belly and hips, finally sliding it between her legs. Her moan became a nearly continuous sob as she waited — waited. Her nerves felt each and every stroke and yet she couldn't move a muscle.

Helpless. This man's toy.

With a start she returned to the present. Mace had pulled her toward him so her legs now dangled off the end of the bed. Her hips only partly rested on the mattress. Despite her fascination with her just-out-of-reach climax, she did her best to accommodate him, spreading her legs wide without waiting for him to signal his wishes. He lowered himself to the ground. Placing his face between her buttocks, he resumed his tongue-play.

If she wanted, she could sit up and put an end to his *invasion* of her private parts. But she didn't. In truth, for the first time in her life, she felt safe with a man's hands — a man's tongue on her pussy.

Fantasy returned. They were still in the orchard, and he'd tied her ankles to nearby trees. Her legs were so far apart she could barely stand, but her roped arms provided the support she needed. Mace glided the vibrator over her labial lips, circled them over and over. She ached to beg him to put it in her but couldn't speak. She existed for his amusement, had become his pet.

His pet, his possession.

A languid heat spread over her. She felt boneless, mindless. Not having to be responsible for her body was wonderful, wonderful! Mace knew what she needed; he'd touch her where she ached to be touched. Under his masterful control she'd—

Her body jerked, and the orchard scene faded. Gasping, she started to close her legs against a sensation so intense it frightened her.

Mace planted his hands over her buttocks and held her in place. After a moment, her trembling quieted enough to allow her to take inventory. Mace's tongue rested against her clit, not moving yet promising—what?

Several more seconds passed. Then he turned his head to the side and sucked. Her consciousness went no further than his warm, damp lips on her clit. A hot wave crashed into her and forced out a long, high cry.

Overwhelmed by the power of her climax, she struggled to find some measure of control, but her muscles had forgotten how to work. She lay limp and useless, drenched in sweat. Mace had stopped sucking her clit, but she felt his breath here, there, and everywhere else on her cunt.

"I can't—" she sobbed. "I need…a minute."

"It's all you're getting."

She was still grappling with his meaning when he slid his tongue into her vagina. At the same time, he captured her pussy lips and spread them. He lapped at her juices, seeming to draw a constant supply out of her.

The heat she'd, maybe, begun to comprehend built once again. Everything tunneled down to sensation. She became aware of each element of her sex, its swollen, sensitive fire. She felt a gathering deep inside, a rolling power.

The wave—the wave! Hot and pure.

Sweat poured from her. She lifted her heavy, throbbing head off the bed and screamed. From the waist down, her body jerked and vibrated. She was exploding, dying!

"Easy, easy. Don't try to move. Just wait, wait and enjoy."

In a disjointed way, she realized she no longer lay on the bed. She must have catapulted herself off it and at Mace because she had no other explanation for why they were both on the floor, he under her and she cradled in his arms. Not sure she could pull it off, she struggled to focus on him.

"That was one hell of a climax," he said.

"I-I guess."

"You guess?"

How could she tell him she'd never experienced something so incredible or frightening?

"What is it?" he asked as her mind whirled.

"I'm scared," she managed. Her body felt boneless, and her brain barely functioned.

"Of me?"

A little. Maybe more than a little. "I think…" She swallowed. "I think I'm afraid of me."

"Don't be." He began massaging her temple. "Sara, you're learning what it is to be a woman, something I'm guessing you never suspected before. Ronnie was all about himself, controlling your body because—hell, he was a sick bastard. Who knows why he did what he—"

"Don't!" she insisted. Shoving away, she struggled to sit up. "Don't talk about him like that!"

"Why not? He's dead."

Is he? Oh God, is he? Before she could summon whatever it would take to answer, she heard a sharp, loud whoosh. A heartbeat later, the mares and their foals squealed. A deep orange light flooded the area of the barn where hay was stored.

Mace and she jumped to their feet as one. "Fire!" he yelled.

"The horses!" She started toward the stalls. "We have to—"

Mace grabbed her and pulled her against him. She felt his clothing on her naked flesh. "I'll get them out," he said, his voice heavy with emotion. "After you're safe."

"No!" From somewhere she managed the strength to break free. "The babies! The babies!"

"All right." He sounded resigned. "Damn, damn! Sara, you need shoes."

He was right of course. Leaving her to find them, he ran toward the mare and foal closest to the already hot-burning hay. The smell of smoke coupled with the animals' growing terror overloaded her senses. She managed to jam her feet into her shoes but didn't take time to dress. Thanks to the awful light cast by the flames, she knew he'd entered the stall and was trying to back the mare into a corner so he could grab her halter.

She ran to the other stall and opened the door, snagging a short length of rope from the top railing at the same time. This mare was trying to place herself between the fire and her baby. Sara looped the rope over her neck.

"Come on, lady. Come on." Although fear clogged her throat, she kept her voice calm as she knotted the rope. "It's all right, nothing to get worried about." She patted the sweating neck and pulled down on the rope, forcing the mare to look at her instead of the fire. "You know me, sweetie. I'm the one who takes care of you, feeds you and keeps your water bucket full and clean. You trust me. Trust."

The moment she had the mare's attention, she tugged on the rope. The foal, whites of its eyes showing, hugged its mother's belly. Although the mare breathed in short, loud bursts, she allowed herself to be led out of the corral. Praying the foal wouldn't panic and run off, Sara kept up her inane chatter, louder now to counter the crackle and snap. She thought she heard Mace, but there was so much noise, she couldn't be sure.

Heat threatened to blister her. Her world consisted of fire and the mare's damp, hot breath on her neck. She'd led horses countless times and would do so tonight.

"Nothing to worry about," she lied as she guided the confused animal one step at a time. Despite the instinct that insisted she run, she kept her pace slow and deliberate. "Just an unscheduled walk when you should have been asleep. Heck of an imposition, I know. I don't much like it either."

Out of the corner of her eye, she saw that the foal had moved behind its dame, so close that the mare's hooves bumped her baby with each step. The poor baby's eyes all but rolled back in its head.

"We'll have to file a protest," she chattered on. The opening was just ahead of them and beyond that, moonlight and safety. *Mace! Where are you?* "You, yanked out of a perfectly good night's sleep, me, interrupted from—well, never mind."

As they passed through the thankfully open barn door, the mare nuzzled her shoulder. Then with a scream born of pent-up terror, the horse reared and bolted, pulling the rope out of Sara's hand. Hot on her tail, the foal too raced for safety.

Sara whirled around. "Mace! Where are you?"

An ominous crackle drew her attention to where she'd first seen the flames. The fire had spread from the hay and was climbing up the barn wall. "Mace!"

A horse screamed, the sound born of panic. Pounding

hooves alerted her just in time to jump to the side as the other mare raced past. She didn't see the foal.

"Mace!" With no thought to her own safety, she headed back inside. Smoke wrapped around her. The heat stole her breath and inflamed her cheeks. She placed her hands over her naked breasts. "Mace! Where are you?"

The heat felt intense, and she was afraid the roof would collapse. She ran back and forth, straining to see through the smoke. She could no longer force his name past her lips, no longer think. Her world boiled down to this raging nightmare.

Mace wouldn't survive. He and the foal he'd risked his life to save would burn to death. She'd have to go on—somehow.

Although she tried to breathe the outside air, she inhaled smoke and started coughing. She was trying to clear her vision when she thought she spotted movement. Wild hope flooded her. She strained to see.

Yes! *Mace.*

He'd thrown the foal over his shoulders and wrapped his arms over the spindly legs to keep from getting kicked. The baby's weight forced him to walk bent over, but as he stepped toward her, he lifted his head. His eyes were red-rimmed, his face flushed.

"You're all right?" he asked.

"Yes." She gripped his arm, then followed him outside. She heard Jerome and Esta yelling but didn't try to get their attention. Instead, she watched as Mace put the foal down. The little one kicked up its hind legs before charging after its mother. Mace started to straighten, then swayed. She wrapped her arm around him and supported him while he coughed.

Finally, he drew a steady breath and started unbuttoning his shirt. "I'm getting you out of here." He pulled off the shirt and wrapped it around her shoulders. "Before it's too late."

"What?"

He began leading her away from the now fiercely burning

143

barn. "He's trying to kill you," Mace said.

Chapter Nineteen

&

The barn was a total loss. Fortunately, by the next afternoon, Jerome had heard from the insurance agent. Except for a small deductible, it and the contents were fully covered. Because they'd been able to use water from the highly productive well, Mace and Jerome had confined the damage to the one structure.

Once she'd assured herself that animals and humans were all right, Esta's biggest fear had been that the buyers would rescind their offer. However, the couple had planned to replace the barn anyway. When they'd asked what had started the fire, Mace had told them what he'd told Jerome and Esta— he'd forgotten to blow out the candle before going to bed. Jerome, who'd seen Sara in his shirt, had muttered something about sleep not being on anyone's mind. But at least the older man had accepted the candle story.

Now, twenty-four hours after the fire, Mace leaned against the corral in the moonlight, watching the two mares and their foals. The one he'd had to manhandle to get out of the barn hadn't yet forgiven him and refused to come near. Fortunately, the other baby didn't associate the male human with last night's fright and was nibbling on his outstretched hand.

"In my next life," Mace told the colt. "I'm coming back as a creature with four legs. One with owners who spoil me and don't expect anything out of me."

He fell silent, his mind going where it needed to go. Sara was helping Esta go through some linens Esta wanted to give to charity. As much as he needed her beside him, he had to be alone to think.

A week ago he would have laughed at the notion of anything paranormal. Now he knew better. True, he'd had Ronnie's evil shoved in his face before he'd met Sara. And from the moment he'd seen the picture of a tied and helpless Sara, he'd comprehended what her husband had been capable of.

You knew before, he reminded himself as the colt wandered off.

Blocking out memories, he focused on the here and now. He shouldn't have come here, but he had. And now Sara was living with the consequences. Yes, so was he, but he didn't give a damn about his own safety.

"You're a bastard," he said, feeling resigned. Ronnie was *here*. He had no doubt of it. "Why do you hate her? What has she ever done to you?"

She's mine.

"No, she isn't," he insisted despite the shock of hearing a dead man. "You don't own her."

She's mine.

"And you're an idiot. She wants nothing to do with you." He debated a moment, then let fire. "She's my lover."

She's mine!

"Give it a rest! Damn it, you spent your whole miserable marriage trying to turn her into—into whatever the hell you wanted her to be. But it didn't work." He tested his surroundings, trying to get a reading on where Ronnie might be. Nothing. "You failed because you couldn't destroy her spirit, her ability to respond the way a woman responds to a man she cares about."

He waited, but Ronnie didn't repeat his insane comment.

"What was last night about?" he demanded. "Were you trying to kill her?" He had to take a calming breath before he could continue. "Do you hate her?"

I love her.

Ronnie Parmenter wasn't capable of the emotion. Just the same, Mace couldn't help but feel sorry for him. "She'll never love you," he said. "Whatever she felt for you at the beginning, you destroyed. You treated her like a sex slave. That isn't love."

She's mine.

"Logic sure as hell isn't your long suit. So you weren't trying to kill her. Then it's me, isn't it?"

You bastard.

"At least we feel the same about each other." How strange it was to be standing surrounded by desert and owls and bats and horses, talking to a dead man and smelling the remnants of smoke—a scent the dead man had been responsible for. "What did you think you'd accomplish by killing me and four innocent horses? What if she'd died?"

No!

On the brink of trying to drum that into Ronnie's head, he changed direction. "Tell me something." He spoke in a conversational tone, two men shooting the breeze. "Who is with you? Wherever you are right now, who's with you?"

No one.

"Ever? Since you died—" He deliberately avoided the word *killed*. "Have you come across another—another presence?"

No.

Despite himself, his thoughts hung up on the loneliness in Ronnie's voice. "In other words, if she died, you're afraid you'll lose her for good. You figure, the only way you can try to rule her is by keeping her alive."

No answer, which was answer in itself.

"I feel sorry for you, Ronnie. I really do." Surprisingly, he did. "But she's fucking me these days, not you. I bring her to climax, not because I force it from her the way you did, but because she trusts her body to me. It's a gift we give each other, not something a captive has no control over."

He didn't want to tell Ronnie these things. Hell, he didn't want to tell Ronnie anything about what went on between him and Sara, but the bastard already knew.

"How do you feel when she screams for me?" He glanced at the house, begging Sara not to come outside. "When she willingly spreads her legs for me?" He should have brought a weapon, but what good was a knife or gun against someone who didn't exist in any way he comprehended? "Tell me something, Ronnie? Did she ever want you to eat her pussy? Did she trust you enough for that, ever?"

Die!

"You'd like that, wouldn't you?" His calm tone stood at contrast to what he felt. If Ronnie could throw a candle into a pile of hay or whatever the hell he'd done, what would stop him from attacking? "For me to be out of her life."

Leave!

"And then what?"

Then she's mine again.

"What if she leaves here?" He wasn't sure where the question came from. "Will you follow her, haunt her no matter where she goes?"

Ronnie said nothing. The dark presence he'd come to accept seemed to fade.

"You're here, aren't you?" he said softly. "But only here."

Leave.

"You don't like me asking hard questions, do you?" The presence had gained a little strength but wasn't as powerful as before. "Forcing the truth from you."

Leave.

"And if I don't? What will you do, kill me?"

I tried.

"And you nearly killed her in the process. I believe you're afraid to try again. And even if you get me and not her, you're afraid you'll destroy something in her — her fight, her will. Without those things, there'll be nothing for you to try to control."

More telling silence followed. The shadowed substance that was Ronnie Parmenter seemed to shudder.

"You've lost," Mace said. He held out his hand and the colt he'd rescued last night stepped toward him. "I've put fire in her. You risk snuffing it out if you kill me. And this is the only place you exist, if that's what it's called." The colt took his fingers into his damp, soft mouth. "Let it go, Ronnie. Let her go."

Chapter Twenty

ॐ

Only half comprehending what she was doing, Sara closed her suitcase and turned to look at her bedroom for the last time.

In the week since the fire, she'd gone through every possible emotion. The sale wouldn't close until the tenth of next month, but instead of staying with Esta and Jerome until then, she and Mace were leaving. The week had been one of frantic activity as the older couple looked for and found a place to buy in Bend, a central Oregon town famous for its outdoor recreation. Although well built, the new place cost considerably less than what they'd get for the farm, leaving with them a nice amount they intended to invest.

She'd felt disloyal leaving early, but Mace had held firm. The sooner she got away, the less chance there was Ronnie would do something else destructive.

"That's all you have?" Mace asked as he came in the room.

"I travel light."

"At least you're traveling." He reached to pick up the suitcase, but instead took her in his arms. "They're going to be all right. The way you've been working to get them ready to move—"

"You've been just as busy." Much as she wanted to stay in his embrace, she pulled free. "Esta is still grumbling over the cost of a moving van, but I think that's because she isn't ready to see me go."

Mace continued to regard her. His fingers had clenched into fists. "You'll see her again. Once you've gotten yourself settled—look, I'd better get out of here. Otherwise, I'm going to be all over you."

They hadn't had sex since the fire. Although she'd been almost desperate for the feel of him, they'd agreed that risking angering Ronnie until she was safely away from his turf was the last thing they wanted to do. Now, staring at Mace's retreating back, she wondered if Ronnie knew what was happening.

He had to. Hadn't he proven how aware he was of everything where she was concerned?

It didn't matter. She was leaving, going where Ronnie couldn't follow. Going with Mace.

* * * * *

After a tearful goodbye and promises to call as soon as they reached Yuba City, Sara got into the passenger seat of her Jeep. Mace turned the vehicle around while she waved at Esta and Jerome, and they started down the long drive.

"I remember when I arrived," Mace said, his voice deep with an emotion she didn't fully fathom. "The wind was blowing. You were hanging clothes on the line."

And you were in Ronnie's car. She'd thought Ronnie's death had ended a chapter in her life, but that time paled in comparison to today. She rolled down her window and turned her face toward the wind. During her marriage, she'd lost touch with the wind. Today it carried promise and memories.

The miles rolled under them. Occasionally one of them said something. The topics were always casual—comments about the news on the radio, observations about the few other drivers, discussion of whether it made more sense to hold onto the Jeep or get a newer one. They stopped for lunch at a café in Prineville, then resumed their westward journey. The terrain began changing from that of high desert to the rich soil that had brought ranchers and farmers to the Willamette Valley.

She'd been here before although in her all but mindless

state, she couldn't recall the details. The longer she spent strapped into her seat with Mace a few inches away, the more she thought about what the two of them would do once they stopped traveling.

Under her, the wheels hummed. The sensation melted into her and left her humming with need. Ever since the barn burned, she'd been afraid of the sexual being in her. Whenever her thoughts stole to memories of the incredible sex she'd shared with Mace, images of flames had rushed over her and silenced desire.

No longer. She was reawakening, feeling like a woman again — the woman Mace had coaxed from her hiding place.

Mace inserted a tape, and the haunting sound of Indian drums and flutes filled the interior. The drums made more of an impact on her senses than the tire sounds had. She couldn't stop from squeezing her thighs together. Her pussy had been empty for so long — a whole week. Pent up need became hungry and demanding.

Heat pressed against her throat and snaked upward, heating her temples, her ears even. She squirmed and clenched her ass. Her fingers dug into the upholstery. The drums continued, the sound growing louder and more frantic like rolling thunder on a stormy night.

In her mind, she spread her legs, and Mace positioned himself between them. He offered no foreplay; she wanted none. He pushed her back, then rammed his cock into her, the invasion hard and urgent. He pounded at her, his thrusts as frantic as the drums. He shoved and shoved again, grunting with each collision of flesh against flesh. She heard herself scream with the rhythm. Her flesh caught fire. The climax rolled out of her, washing like a massive wave. Joyous, she dove into the fiery current.

The car was slowing, tires now crunching over gravel. Trying not to breathe like a racehorse, she focused on Mace. His attention was on the unpaved road he'd turned onto.

"What are you doing?" she asked.

"I don't think I need to spell it out."

The long unused track snaked through scrub oaks. When Mace stopped and turned off the engine, she couldn't hear the vehicles from the highway they'd left. Not looking at her, he exited and came over to her side of the car. When he opened the door, she got out, then stood there, shaking.

He didn't speak as he unfastened her jeans and tugged them off her hips. He didn't need to because the bulge in his jeans said everything. Still silent, he bent her over the front bumper. After taking off her shoes and jeans, he positioned her so her legs were widely splayed — as they'd been in her fantasy a few minutes before.

He freed his swollen and red cock, leaving his jeans around his ankles. When he ran his hands under her shirt and pushed on her ribcage, she placed her hands behind her to support her upper body. He stepped into the space between her legs. His cock expertly found and kissed her hot, wet cunt lips.

She needed to say something, anything, but what? She simply wanted to be fucked. Mace clamped his hands over her thighs, then, still silent, he pushed his cock into her opening. The sensation of being filled, of the end to a week of empty hunger rushed through her. She flung her head back and closed her eyes.

There. Nothing but a cunt. Existing only between her legs. Mace's cock claiming her pussy, his thrusts vibrating through her. Her clit, the so small, so powerful piece of flesh grew hotter and hotter. By using her feet on the bumper for leverage, she rhythmically lifted her buttocks off the hard metal and pulled his cock deeper into her. Drums and flutes had become as one in the ancient Indian musical chant. The same thing was happening between her and Mace.

She pushed and retreated, pushed and retreated. Her thigh and calf muscles strained. Her head felt as if it would burst, but she didn't care.

He started to shudder, not just his cock but maybe his entire being. Even as she lost control, she traced and recorded each nuance of his sexual release. She felt his cum shoot into her, imagined her flesh drinking of his gift.

Intent on pumping her legs and ass, she was slow to capture her own climax's initial wave. By the time she comprehended it was happening, sanity was lost. She opened her eyes and stared up into the trees. Exploded. Her feet bounced off the bumper. She would have slipped off the hood if Mace's cock hadn't held her in place.

* * * * *

"No," Mace said when she reached for her panties and jeans.

She gave him a questioning look, but he only picked them and her shoes up and threw them into the back seat.

"Get in," he said.

"What? I can't—"

"I've kept my hands off you long enough." He opened the passenger door. "I want your pussy where I can get to it."

"You want—what?"

"Don't." He grabbed her wrists. Pulling her against him, he drew her hands behind her and pressed them into her naked buttocks. "Don't pretend you don't need this as much as I do."

Damn, damn, damn, he was right. Although the admission shook her, she didn't object when he pushed her into the Jeep and fastened the shoulder harness around her. Anyone they encountered on the highway would see a casually dressed couple in a 4-wheel drive rig. Only she and Mace would know the woman in the passenger's seat was naked from the waist down.

She kept her legs together as he returned to the highway.

They remained like that for maybe ten miles as he concentrated on the increasing traffic. She'd begun to relax just a little, to think about the hard and frantic fuck back in the oaks when she felt his right hand on her left thigh. Swallowing, she glanced over at him. He looked back.

"I don't know if Ronnie's treatment was responsible or whether there's always been a part of you that responds to manhandling." His hand slid between her legs. Then he turned it into a fist and shoved against her inner thighs, spreading her. "You like it hard, don't you?"

She looked down at herself, seeing her red and still-swollen pussy lips. She felt her own juice and some of Mace's cum remaining in her slide out.

"I-I don't know."

"Yes, you do." He took her lips between thumb and forefinger and squeezed them together. She was still trying to keep up with her cunt's reaction when he began sliding the so sensitive pieces of flesh against each other. "You just haven't allowed yourself to admit it, Sara." He drew her lips away from her body, creating a delicious tension. "There's nothing wrong with any reaction you have. You're a healthy, sexual being."

He released her labial lips but slipped his middle finger inside her before she understood the momentary freedom.

His finger lay quiet inside her. Anticipating, needing, her pussy muscles clenched at him. He chuckled and stroked her inner walls, once. "This is what I'm talking about, Sara. You feeling free to explore your sexuality. To want to let go of the control you fought so long for."

His finger curled toward the spot Ronnie had once laid claim to, the needy and sometimes hated G-spot her husband had used to control her. *You can trust this man*, a voice inside her said. *He isn't Ronnie. Ronnie is dead, his essence back at the ranch – trapped in that lonely place. Unable to get at you.*

Relishing her freedom, she scooted toward Mace, spread

her legs even more, laid the back of her head against the seat, and closed her eyes. Her consciousness faded until she knew nothing except his finger inside her.

He reached and stroked, easily found the core of sensation. She couldn't tell whether his finger pad or nail touched her there, didn't care about anything except the sweet, hot lightning bolt.

His touch came and went so fast she'd think she'd imagined it if not for her reaction. She seemed capable of an endless flood and couldn't keep her ass on the seat. When reaching toward him failed to bring her G-spot and his finger back in contact, she pushed her ass as far into the seat as possible.

There! Another touch! Here and gone in a heartbeat.

"Mace!"

"Be patient, Sara. Be a little less hungry."

But she couldn't obey him, not when the primitive creature within her cried out, demanding attention.

As the miles rolled under them, she lost all touch with reality. In a dim way she comprehended that afternoon was turning into night, long shadows spreading over the world and wrapping them in darkness. They left the two-lane highway and joined the vehicles charging up and down I-5, the state's freeway. Lights occasionally penetrated the car's interior but not her consciousness.

Except when they were in heavy traffic or on a winding stretch of road, Mace's hand lived between her legs. She wanted him in her always, his fingers filling her to bursting, pushing the hidden trigger that brought her to the brink of climax. But he played the game—if that's what it was—his way. Oh, he kept her wonderfully stimulated but reaching the edge over and over again was exhausting.

Once, desperate to have her clit stroked, she'd grabbed his wrist and tried to direct him. Instead of letting her have her way, he'd ordered her to slide her hands under her thighs and keep them there. Buying into the fantasy of helplessness fed her hunger. Maybe she could have debated his earlier question of whether she'd always wanted to be controlled, but she preferred just existing.

She wasn't sure where they were when he pulled off the freeway. Feeling disjointed, she sat up.

"We need gas," he said.

"Mace." She pulled her legs together for the first time in maybe hours. "They'll see me."

"No they won't." He reached behind him, grabbed her jeans, and draped them over her crotch.

She sat staring ahead but not really seeing anything while Mace bought gas. Then, although they hadn't discussed it, he went through a drive-thru for hamburgers and drinks. They'd finished eating before they'd put Eugene's city limits behind them.

Instead of resuming his sex-play, he turned on the radio and tuned in a high school basketball game. Although she didn't understand why he'd care, he seemed fascinated by the lopsided score. Her jeans remained on her lap.

"We're going to spend the night in Ashland," he said after a long silence. "There's a park there I'm taking you to."

"A park?"

"It's several thousand acres and much of it follows a creek. There are duck ponds, playgrounds, open areas, private places."

Private places. "What if I don't want to go there?"

"It doesn't matter. I do."

If her husband had said that, she would have been terrified. Instead, thoughts of what Mace planned to do with and to her instantly reawakened the part of her the basketball game and a full belly had started to lull.

"And because I'm in charge, there's something you're going to do now to get us ready," he said.

Chapter Twenty-One

ଈ

Mace remained silent. Waiting for him, Sara's thoughts swung from the modern freeway taking them south to a new life, the night air that might soon turn so cold she'd have to wind up the window, the endless trucks, the bored sounding basketball announcer. She should wonder how Esta and Jerome were handling their first night alone, but they belonged to a world she barely recalled.

"Put your right hand between your legs."

Startled, she could only stare over at Mace.

"You heard me. Right hand, between your legs."

"What—"

"No, no talking. Not until I tell you to. Do it, Sara."

Sara. She loved the way he said her name, like fireflies on a breeze. Opening her legs a little, she rested her hand where he'd commanded.

"Now put your left hand on the inside of my thigh."

That she could do, no problem. She wondered what it would take to distract him from driving, then decided to leave that up to him. Tonight everything was under his direction, most of all her.

"Two fingers inside yourself, Sara. Middle and forefinger. Slow and easy, fingers curved. Scrunch down if you have to but don't take your hand off me."

She had to put most of her weight on her spine before she could get her fingers all the way in.

"Just keep them there for awhile," he said. "Don't move them."

"I don't know if—"

"Did I say you could talk?"

She shook her head and concentrated on the seemingly impossible act of simply resting her fingers in her cunt. It became even harder when he pinched her left nipple through two layers of fabric. He kept the pressure going, shutting off her circulation—as had happened when Ronnie had put clamps there. Despite the unwanted comparison, her sexual awareness kicked up a notch.

He began rubbing her nipple between his fingers, forcing a gasp from her. "It doesn't hurt, Sara. I'd never hurt you. But tonight, by the time we reach the park, you're going to be so ready, you're going to want to rape me. And I won't be far behind—a bit because we don't need an accident. Feel this." He pulled on her nipple. "Feel it all the way to your belly."

She did, her concentration causing her head to roll toward him. Her fingers on his thigh pressed into his flesh.

"Now use your cunt fingers to try to reach your belly."

At first she couldn't make sense of what he'd told her. Then logic kicked in. Lifting her hips a little, she pressed inward. Her own flesh against his flesh wasn't as exciting as him manipulating her, yet she couldn't complain.

"Wiggle them. Back and forth, back and forth. Run your nails along your pussy walls. Are you doing that?"

She nodded, then realized he couldn't see her in the dark so relayed her obedience by pressing against his thigh.

"Good girl. Keep it going. Back and forth, then side to side. Spread your fingers as much as you can, push against your cunt and think about my swollen cock in there. Do you feel my cock, Sara, do you?"

She nodded, then again pressed her fingertips into his flesh. Her fingers threatened to slip out of her drenched pussy, but he hadn't given her permission to stop, and she'd do what he commanded for as long as he said. She would, she could.

"Take it down a notch, Sara. Back off a bit. It isn't time to go over the edge, not yet."

The edge. With his fingers claiming her left nipple and her own fingers monopolizing her cunt until he could take over, she was a half step from falling into space.

"Down a notch. Slow those fingers."

Much as she wanted to do the opposite, she sent the orders to her hand until her fingers barely glided over her hot and slick pussy.

"Good. I'm going to let go of your breast now because it isn't the most comfortable or safe position for me to be in. From now on, you'll be doing all the work."

She couldn't imagine what he had in mind and could hardly wait for what was to come next.

"Two fingers fit pretty easy, don't they?" he asked.

She pressed.

"Now we're going to find out what you can accomplish with three."

Apprehension snaked down her spine.

"Do it, Sara. Get your ring finger in on the act."

I can do this. I will do this. For you.

The insertion took more than a little contorting on her part, but by leaning toward him, she managed to fill her opening.

"Crowded in there, is it?"

She pressed.

"A little hard accomplishing much movement?"

Another press.

"That's all right, for now. Just keep them in there. Spread yourself a bit so I won't have trouble getting in. Now, I want you to slide your hand from my thigh to under my balls. Don't do more than that because we don't want me running off the road, but I don't want you having all the fun. Slow and easy, Sara. Slow and easy and remember, don't take your fingers out of yourself."

She had to all but rest her head on his lap in order to wrap her hand under his balls. Although the shoulder harness cut into her, she lifted her right leg onto the seat, thus assuring continued access to her pussy.

Mace said nothing as the miles hummed under them. The basketball game had ended and been replaced by country and western music.

She couldn't say she was deeply aroused. Awkwardness prevented that. But she loved feeling part of both herself and him, touching him and her in an intimate way. Night kept her thoughts from going elsewhere. He wanted her cunt ready for him. She needed the same readiness in his sexual organs and for him to want nothing except to fuck her tonight—and every other night.

Images of endless nights with his cock buried in her snagged her attention. Much as she relished being part of him, she wasn't sure she could handle it. Almost from the first time Ronnie had fucked her, she'd struggled to divorce herself from the act. Could she change? But if she didn't, what would her future be? Yes, she'd go to college and start a career, find a place to live and coax life from the land, but was it enough?

No. The answer transmitted itself through her clit. Becoming part of Mace had altered her, shifted her in ways she couldn't have anticipated.

"Easy," Mace muttered. "Just cradle me for now."

Brought back to reality, she forced her fingers to ease up. She continued to support his balls, but after a few more miles, a cramp developed in her neck.

"Mace? I can't keep this up."

He sighed and patted her head. "I know. It was fantastic while it lasted." After another pat, he pulled her hand off him. She straightened but managed to keep her fingers in her pussy. If she removed the seatbelt and got down on the floor on her knees, she could take his cock in her mouth—and cause an accident.

"I have to go to the bathroom," he said. "What about you?"

"Yes," she admitted. "I'll put my jeans—"

"No, not yet."

She remained silent as he moved into the right lane and took an unlit exit. They were in the mountains with evergreens growing all around, the air crisp. He crept along until lights from the freeway were no longer visible, then parked on the shoulder.

"Shoes back on," he told her. "Use the napkins from our dinner."

Beset by a mix of apprehension over being discovered and the delicious sense of doing something forbidden, she disengaged her fingers from her weeping pussy, slipped into her shoes, and hurried into the woods. She squatted and relieved herself, then returned to the car and got in. Her ass and legs had gotten cold, causing her to shiver. Mace was doing something in the trunk, and she rubbed warmth back into her thighs while she waited. Would he want her to go back to stretching her opening?

He came around to her side of the car and opened the door. "I found some things in the trailer," he said. "Some things I'm sure belonged to Ronnie."

Apprehension tightened her throat. "What?"

"Sex toys, although I doubt if either of you saw them as toys." He brought one hand into view, letting her see the large red vibrator with numerous rubbery knobs on the hard surface. "Did he use it on you?"

"Once." She shivered. "The batteries didn't last long. Besides, he found a-a bigger one he liked better."

"I saw it, burned it. Have you tried this on yourself?"

She shook her head and forced herself not to drop her gaze.

"I'd like you to tonight, but it has to be your decision."

Staring at the vibrator, she tried to go back to when Ronnie had commanded her to spend the day with it rammed inside her, but because Mace held it, the memory faded. "You have fresh batteries?" she asked.

"Yes."

Sighing, she scrunched forward on the seat and spread her legs, watched him insert it. For a moment it lay unmoving in her pussy. Then he turned the dial, and it began humming.

"It'll go higher."

"All right."

He made another adjustment. She felt as if she was vibrating from knees to belly button.

"Like it?" he asked.

"Yes."

"Fresh batteries." He kissed her. "It'll last all the way to Ashland."

She couldn't hold her head up, couldn't keep her eyes open. Heat had already flooded her pussy. Fresh juice leaked around the object, threatening to allow it to slide out. Determined to hold it in place, she closed her legs. He fastened her seatbelt and lifted her arms so her hands were behind her head.

"Pretend you've been tied up," he said. He rubbed her belly, hard, as if trying to touch the vibrator. "Only this time it was done by someone you trust."

"I-I trust...you."

When he said nothing, she opened her eyes to find him leaning over her. His hand still pressed her belly. In the dark she couldn't read his expression but heard his deep breathing.

* * * * *

No matter how firmly he told himself not to look at Sara,

Mace couldn't keep his eyes off her. When he'd found the vibrator, his first impulse had been to burn the damn thing. But a number of his past sex partners had loved them. If he could help Sara see that what had been an instrument of domination in one man's hand could be a gift of love from another —

Love.

The word buried itself inside him. He should find a way to rid himself of it, to deny its existence. After all, if Sara learned the truth about him, she might come to hate him.

Sara, hate?

Because that question seemed easier to face than whether he'd fallen in love with her, he stole another glance at her. She hadn't changed position although her legs looked tightly clamped. Her breathing was ragged.

He thought about again asking if she was enjoying herself, but he'd have to be a fool not to be able to figure that out. Just imagining what she must feel ratcheted up his erection. He'd never been in such a hurry to get somewhere in his life. As for what he hoped would happen once they were in the park —

Smiling ruefully, he tried to concentrate on his agenda for the rest of the night, but the ache in his groin kept distracting him. He'd indulged in some minor bondage play with two girlfriends but hardly considered himself an expert. Sara might balk at anything more than what they'd done so far, but if she admitted she enjoyed it — with him playing the master role, of course — who knew where this might lead. Maybe, if he was lucky, they'd never get around to discussing anything else.

Like his role in Ronnie's murder.

Sara shifted position. Without taking his eyes off the road, he ran his hand between her legs and pulled up on the vibrator so it pressed against the back of her pussy. She half rose off the seat, then settled down again.

He loved her. No way about it, he loved this vulnerable

and sexy woman. She trusted him. That was the hell of it, she trusted him.

For how long?

* * * * *

Sara barely roused from her sex-stupor when Mace exited the freeway. She scrunched down so hopefully no one could see her, but he had positioned her this way, and she wanted to please him. He entered a surface street, then drove around to the back of a modern looking motel.

"Stay here," he said as he opened his door. "I'll get us a room."

Stay here with a vibrator stuck up your pussy and nothing on from the waist down. The image made her laugh. Her amusement faded, replaced by a vague discomfort. She brought her arms down and rubbed them until they tingled. She hadn't intended to fiddle with the vibrator but wound up doing just that. Mace had positioned it so it pressed against the back of her pussy, causing that area to become so sensitive it was almost painful. She tried shifting it forward in hope of reaching her G-spot, but the vibrator was straight and missed the so-sensitive area.

Never mind. Her clit was equally sensitive. She wasn't sure Mace would approve of her removing the toy, but if he frowned, she'd explain she was just keeping herself at a fever pitch for him.

Explain. She'd never been able to do that with Ronnie, never wanted to be sexually excited around him.

A little unnerved by the changes in her since Mace entered her life, she nevertheless set her mind to a little clit-titillation. She'd directed the tip of the vibrator to the perfect spot and had started pressing when a sharp sound stopped her.

Frightened, she sat upright.

Mace stared in at her.

"I have the room," he said. "But we're not going in until later."

"We aren't?" she managed. The vibrator hummed against her clit.

"No. First, the park."

Chapter Twenty-Two

&

Sara took in the lush, beautifully maintained park. There'd been muted but effective lights at the most public parts, but they were now driving slowly along a dark, narrow track of road. If it hadn't been for the moon and car lights, she couldn't have seen anything. Despite her fascination with a land far different from the arid country where she'd grown up, she realized she hadn't seen any other vehicles for maybe five minutes. The car clock said 9:15 p.m..

"We'll come back in the morning before we leave," Mace said, "so you can see it in the light. Nature has been nurtured here."

"It's incredible." The vibrator continued to hum but now with less strength as the batteries ran down. Mace's hand rested on the inside of her thigh, providing its own stimulation. "Just thinking about what's possible given enough water and a less harsh climate—"

"It's like that where I live, Sara." He pulled into a shadowed turnout and killed the engine. "You're going to love working with plants you've never been able to before."

She really was moving, wasn't she—turning her life around—committing to a future with this man she'd fallen in love with. Trying to make her peace with reality took her full attention. She didn't realize Mace had gotten out until he opened her door. Instead of helping her out, he placed his hand around her throat and gently pushed her against the back of the seat.

"I want to try something," he told her. "I believe you need and are ready for this, but if it makes you at all uncomfortable, let me know."

"What…what will you be doing?"

Still holding onto her neck, he reached between her legs and pulled out the dying vibrator. He held it where they could both see it. "You have the soul of a submissive. Around the right man, a man you trust, you can express that side of you. You'll come to love turning your body over to a man. But it's a delicate balance, one we need to work at."

If she wanted, she could have pulled Mace's hand off her throat, but she didn't. "Are you saying that because it's the only way you can figure I stayed with Ronnie?"

He placed the vibrator on the seat beside her, then quickly, surely slid two fingers up her pussy. "We aren't going to talk about him tonight."

Wonderful.

"This is about us, our exploration of our relationship." He pressed, just like that igniting her clit. "Tell me if it's what you want."

"I…want."

"Good."

She hoped he'd finger-fuck her right here in the car. Instead, he released her and ordered her to get out. Shaking a little in anticipation, she planted her legs under her. He folded his arms across his chest and stared down at her. "Take off your shirt," he said.

His words slid over her skin before seeping through layers of being. She heard an owl, frogs, crickets, water from a creek hidden deep in the vegetation. The smell was rich and moist, endless growing things gifting her with their essence. She felt part of the trees, plants, and grasses, part of Mace. No flicker of fear touched her, only anticipation and the gift of surrender.

Head bowed, she unfastened her shirt and left it on the hood. Then she removed her bra. A breeze licked her breasts and lifted and hardened them.

"Good," he said. "Now lean over the hood as far as you

can, arms outstretched."

She wasn't sure how she felt about not being able to see him but did as he said. He left her there for a moment while he got something out of the trunk. When she sensed his presence behind her, she started to turn.

"No. Close your eyes."

She did as he'd commanded and found herself locked in sensation, no longer distracted by her surroundings. She'd placed her hands above her head and kept them limp as he wrapped a rope around her right wrist. He drew first it and then her other arm behind her back, then tied her hands together, leaving enough slack so she felt no tension in her shoulders. He took hold of her shoulders and helped her stand. Next he placed another soft rope around her neck and tied it, leaving a length to dangle between her breasts and down her legs.

"I found the rope in the trailer," he told her. "There were some hairs on them, same color as yours."

"He, ah, he…"

"I know. At least I can guess. The difference this time is there won't be any pain—at least no more than you want."

She needed to look him in the eye for yet more reassurance, but he hadn't given her permission. When he took hold of the loose rope and ran it between her legs, she stood with her knees locked, waiting, wanting. He tied it to the rope restraining her wrists. The loop between her legs dangled, not touching her cunt. Next he took hold of the loop and did something with it. Then he told her to open her eyes.

He'd tied yet another rope to what was between her legs and held that end. Instead of explaining his intention, he demonstrated by pulling on the end. The soft cotton between her legs tightened, pressing against her labia.

"Your leash," he said.

He used the contraption to lead her down a footpath. The cotton imprisoned her labia, and with each step, the harness glided over her clit, distracting her from her surroundings. The hard bud pulsed. Her passage flooded, but the rope kept the moisture trapped inside.

She felt like a walking cunt. She didn't care where they went and couldn't think ahead to what might happen once he reached his destination. He hadn't said whether he'd ever been down this path before, not that it mattered. He was her master.

When he slowed, she tried to see what he was looking at but couldn't find her way past the crashing sensations. She'd lost control of her hands. A rope much like ones she'd put around countless horses circled her neck to remind her of her enslavement.

Mostly she felt the drag and pull of cotton against her sex. It didn't matter that she'd allowed this to happen. She'd given herself, her body, over to this big, dark man. Every fiber in her begged for more.

"There," he said. He didn't explain further but hauled her over to a couple of trees about five feet apart. He positioned her between them, then released her and took hold of the rope he'd looped over his shoulder. As he unwound it, she marveled at its length. He had enough rope for—for what?

She waited as he untied her left wrist and shook the crotch rope off the short length on her right wrist. The crotch rope dropped, freeing her cunt. Fluid gushed from her to run down her inner thighs. She belatedly realized he'd pulled her right arm up and out and was fastening it to one of the trees. Once he'd secured her, he did the same to her left arm so she now stood between the trees, caught to them. She could still bend her elbows slightly.

Next he used the extra rope to tie her ankles in the same way as he'd done her wrists, pulling her legs apart so the night air moved freely over her sex. The faint breeze felt cold on her juice-dampened labia.

He stepped back, examining his handiwork. In the moonlight he was little more than shadow and shape, and in her brain, her being even, he became a dangerous and powerful stranger. She was his just-captured prisoner. He could and would do everything he wanted with her.

Fiery feathers of sensation spread from her throat, over her breast, scraped along her belly and settled hot and heavy throughout her pussy. She wanted to close her eyes so she could concentrate, but she needed to watch the dangerous stranger.

Maybe he could smell her. Maybe he felt her heat. Whatever she'd given away, he tested her reaction by sliding his fingers over her labia. Washed and slick with her juices, they glided easily. She felt awash in fluid, but he managed to take hold of her lips and pull down. She straightened and drew away from him, increasing the pull.

"Helpless is good, Sara," he muttered. "Helpless is trust."

Before she could think what to do with his wisdom, he closed his mouth over her right breast and began sucking. He stopped pulling on her labia and ran first one, then two, and finally three fingers in her pussy.

She lost touch, lost control. He became her everything, ruler and guide. Her belly clenched, and she tried to close her legs so she could trap him inside her. He chuckled at her futile efforts, his breath hot on her breast.

After a moment, he started sucking again. When he began rotating his palm from side to side, pressing against her cunt, she sensed a clawing, growing climax.

Because he'd left her with some freedom of movement, she sagged down as far as she could, desperate to suck his fingers deep inside her throbbing passage. He didn't try to stop her and answered her demand with one of his own. He pressed and rotated, his skin so wet she could barely distinguish between her flesh and his.

All of a sudden, she felt something approaching pain on her free breast. He'd grabbed her nipple and was twisting and pulling. Her moan caught in her throat. He closed his teeth over the other nipple, teased and tasted.

Her thighs burned. Her knees and calves felt like rubber. The ropes pulled on her wrists, but she didn't care. Let her be stretched out. She was, she was—

"I'm coming!" she sobbed.

Just as the first wonderful wave caught her, she felt his fingers suck out of her. Sensation fled her breasts. Disoriented, she struggled to straighten.

He stood back from her, features stern and moon-shadowed.

"Not yet," he said. "Not until I'm ready for you to."

Just like that, she hated him with every fiber in her. Her pussy muscles continued to spasm, forcing her to draw her legs together as much as possible. Perhaps he knew what she was thinking because he dropped to his knees where darkness sheltered him. She was leaning toward him, both loathing and relishing the strain in her arms when he straightened. He held yet more rope.

She watched him approach, felt his impact on her breasts and belly. He closed his hand around the lead dangling from her neck, draped it under a breast and wound it behind her back. He brought it around to the front and over the already roped breast. He fastened it in place by looping the end over her arm and tying it. Then, saying nothing, explaining nothing, he tied the new rope to the back of her cotton leash and circled her body over and over. He left slack in the loops, but she still felt the cotton over and under both breasts, around her waist, down her legs.

No longer hating him, she waited for him to snug it on her crotch as he'd done when he was leading her here, but he left her free there.

"Beautiful," he said when he was done. "Even in the moonlight, I can see the contrast between your flesh and white rope. You're mine and yet you aren't. One word and I'll let you go. You understand, don't you?"

She nodded. *His. Her body belonged to him.* The thought nearly brought her to climax again.

"I know you do," he whispered. "I just wanted to lay out the boundaries again."

He studied her for what seemed a long time. She continued to lose herself in waves of pleasure and waited for what he'd do next. Instead of touching her, he disappeared into the woods. She wasn't afraid he'd leave her like this, but the fantasy of helplessly waiting for his return added to the delicious heat.

Mace was right. She'd hated her husband's cruel domination, but she'd long wanted to explore the submissive side to her nature. Perhaps in some perverted way, she'd stayed with Ronnie as long as she had because she'd been waiting for him to turn pain into pleasure, to allow her to enjoy restraint as much as he'd relished restraining.

She loved this! Loved being Mace's possession!

When Mace returned, he'd stripped out of his clothes. Moonlight touched his flesh, revealing his hard muscles and insistent cock. Slow and measured, he walked up to her, crouched, and ran his cock along her lips. "I want to keep you like this always," he told her. "To have you accessible to me whenever I want—for both of us."

The image caused her to pant. She arched her back, straining to bring her crotch closer to him. For an awful second, she thought he'd deny her. Then he dropped to his knees and turned her, giving his mouth full access to her pussy.

She couldn't see anything and could no longer hear. She felt only his tongue on her lips. He bathed her with a mix of their fluids, circled her labia as earlier he'd circled her body with rope. No matter how much she wanted to remain still for him, her legs closed as much as the ropes allowed. Then, prodded by his tongue, she opened them again—wider this time.

He used his fingers to separate her lips, and although she knew what was coming, she jumped and sobbed when he slid his tongue into her vagina. She felt him lap at her fluids and gave him what seemed like an endless supply. Thank god for the ropes. Otherwise, she would have jumped him.

In her mind, she placed him in chains. He became the helpless prisoner waiting for his mistress to service him, to rape him if she so desired.

Would it be rape? The sight of her naked body alone would fill his cock with blood. He'd strain toward her and beg to be allowed in her velvet cave.

And she was a kind and knowing mistress. She'd grant him enough freedom so he could work his cock between her legs. She'd use something, maybe a rope around his neck, to control the speed and timing of his trusts. Drawing out his release, delaying it, sometimes denying him — those things became her pleasure. Despite other demands on her time, she'd never forget her sex slave. She'd come to him each night, loosen his chains and —

But she was the helpless one. And Mace controlled her sex, not the other way around.

Sweat snaked down her sides. Her cheeks felt on fire. Her thighs contracted, released, contracted again. Her breathing rasped, and he milked her over and over, took her clit between his teeth and held it as her body jerked. Her bit of flesh flamed and ached and became a wild beast intent on receiving pleasure, hating and loving the constraint on it at the same time.

When it became too much, she fought to free her throbbing clit from what might become endless punishment. At the same time, she dove into the incredible sensation and became it. She shuddered; the tremor flowed throughout her, touched her everywhere, melted into her bonds.

"Not yet, Sara, not yet."

"Bastard!" she sobbed. When she looked down, he was no

longer between her legs.

She wasn't sure how long he was gone this time. When he returned, he carried two large rocks. Not looking at her, he placed them near her feet and helped her stand on them. Then he loosened the ropes around her ankles.

He placed one hand at the small of her back and pulled her toward him. His hand stole lower to slide between her ass cheeks. One finger moved to her pussy, and he stroked her vagina.

"Enough play, my pet. It's time for my reward."

Mine too.

He gripped her buttocks and forced her even closer. With the rocks under her, his cock and her cunt were now in perfect alignment. She helped by straining her lower body toward him and leaning back at the waist. He kept his hands on her, secured her as his cock glided into her wet and willing opening.

He might have been gentle in the past, but tonight he took her hard and fast, sweating and grunting with each urgent thrust. Without his support, she would have lost her purchase. But he held her, helped her, gave her the necessary support so she could meet each assault.

His balls slapped into her as he rammed and rammed again. Made wild by the lengthy foreplay, she came before he did, muscles straining and powerful, teeth clenched, breasts swaying in time to the mutual assault. Her body jumped and shivered and danced in time with her sobs.

She felt him crouch and gather himself. When he ran himself full and hard into her, she met him head on.

"Fuck me, fuck me, fuck me," she chanted.

She thought her climax had spent itself and felt her muscles start to relax. Then a volcano erupted. She yanked on the ropes, twisting and turning so the loops scraped over her flesh. He remained lodged in her, skewering her, balancing her on his cock.

"Damn you. Damn you," he chanted.

She barely heard him.

Chapter Twenty-Three

❧

After releasing her bonds, Mace threw Sara over his shoulder and carried her back to the car. She could have walked, but he wasn't ready to end the fantasy. He felt her breasts on his back, and although he felt wrung out, he risked a repeat performance by sliding his hand up an inner thigh, along her sopping and swollen pussy, then down the other. She muttered something and all but dislodged herself trying to capture his hand when he repeated the journey.

He put her back in the car, placed the vibrator on her lap, and returned for his clothes and the ropes. By then exertion and night air had returned him to sanity. Holding the white cotton at arms' length, he cursed himself.

He didn't regret what he'd done. Mastering her had taken them both to a place they needed to go. She'd needed to meet and embrace this element of her nature. Hopefully, the ropes would free her emotionally and she could step into the future, kill the past.

"Can she?" he asked himself. "Or will you make that impossible."

Putting back on his clothes and driving out of the park did nothing to silence the question. Sara didn't speak, and he suspected she too was trying to come to grips with what they'd done. She might think her reasons for willingly exploring yet more bondage were complex, but they were nothing compared to what he had to wrestle with—what might happen once he'd taken her to where Ronnie had died.

They didn't have sex again that night—they'd been too tired—but they made up for it the next morning. He'd been waking up when he'd felt her fingers on his cock. She'd let him

177

go to the bathroom but had been waiting for him when he returned. She hadn't exactly jumped his bones but came close by pressing him onto the mattress before straddling him and skewering herself on him. They'd rolled over and nearly fallen off the bed, and she'd laughed, delighting him with the sound of freedom.

After a leisurely breakfast, they'd gotten on the road and driven through to Yuba City, reaching his place in early afternoon.

"You live here?" she asked. She'd gotten out of the car but hadn't made a move toward the isolated house.

"For the past five years. It came with the orchard." He nodded at the dark, almond-laden trees growing on three sides of the small but sturdy ranch style house with its large front porch. "It keeps me close to my work and out of the city."

"Alone?"

"For the most part, yes."

He'd been ready to take her hand and guide her inside, but she started forward. He couldn't tell whether she approved or whether she had doubts about being here. Watching her, he longed to freeze them in this moment. He wouldn't have to take over responsibility for the orchard. She wouldn't begin the process of enrolling in college. She wouldn't meet his sister or see where Ronnie's blood had spilled.

Most of all, he wouldn't risk her hatred.

Sara sensed Mace's reluctance to join her but didn't understand. He'd been quiet and distracted today, and she'd had to remind herself he wasn't capable of the same dark moods that sometimes had turned Ronnie into a monster. No matter what was on Mace's mind, he wouldn't hurt her.

She stood aside so he could unlock the front door, then followed him inside. The interior smelled musty, and he opened several windows. They left the door open.

This was a man's house, a place of dark leather and

simple decorations, hardwood floors and a small, utilitarian kitchen. She glanced into his bedroom long enough to note the double bed under a navy spread. If she lived here, if they both wanted that, would they buy a larger one?

"I'll get our things in a few minutes," he said. "First I need to check my messages and probably make some calls."

"Fine. I need to use the bathroom."

Like the rest of the house, the bathroom served a man who spent little time inside. She wondered if he'd let her buy some new towels, and if she was ready to put her stamp on the place.

By the time she returned to the living room, Mace was on the phone. It sounded business-related so she went out to the car and brought in their suitcases. She didn't want to put her things in his closet without consulting him so unpacked his suitcase and went back to the living room.

He was still on the phone and mouthed that she should find something for them to eat. To her surprise, she found fresh milk and vegetables. Who had stocked these things?

"My sister," Mace explained when he joined her as she was scrambling eggs. "I told her when I'd be back."

"She lives nearby?"

"About ten miles away." He leaned against the counter and studied her. "I like seeing you in here."

Something about his tone caught her attention, and she turned toward him. That's all it took. Yes, they'd fucked thoroughly this morning. Yes, something about his sister was responsible for his somber expression, but he wanted her here.

Stepping close, she wrapped her arms around his waist. "I'm glad to be here."

"Forever?"

Heavy. Much too heavy. Avoiding the question, she stood on tiptoe and kissed him deeply. He pulled her close and held her against his hardening cock. She couldn't have broken free if she'd tried, but she didn't want to; at least she told herself she didn't. Denying a finger of distrust and near fear, she focused on her sexual response. Certainly he had things to do, but maybe they could wait. And via the act of sex, she could silence her...her what?

Her calves threatened to cramp, and she tried to settle down on her feet, but he refused to let her. Instead, he continued to vise her against him. His cock expanded and his breathing was quick. Some bondage play last night had been fine, but she didn't want it today. She wanted—

"Mace? What are you doing?" She had to wrench her head to the side to ask. "You're hurting me."

"I don't want to," he muttered. His grip loosened but only slightly. "But I can't—"

A loud gasp stopped Mace. She'd thought his muscles were tense before, but as he turned toward the feminine sound, he became like steel. He continued to hold her and trap her within his strength.

A young woman stood at the open front door. She was casually dressed and slightly built with long, limp hair and old eyes. Her mouth was drawn into a hard line. Despite her clenched jaw, Sara sensed a soul-deep vulnerability. *A girlfriend, a lover?*

"You should have knocked," Mace said.

"No, I shouldn't," the woman replied. She took a step, then stopped. The way she'd clamped her arms around her middle made Sara wonder if she was sick. Now that she was closer, Sara could see how pale she looked. She wore no makeup but was pretty enough that she really didn't need any. There was a porcelain doll quality to her, fragile and breakable—maybe already broken.

After a long, awkward silence, the woman started forward again. She swayed, and Mace released Sara and hurried to her side. The woman sagged and let him guide her to the couch. She slumped in it, then straightened and stared at

Sara.

A lightning bolt of recognition shot through Sara. She'd seen this woman before, somewhere, the matter of their meeting dark and tangled. She didn't believe she knew her name but understood deeply the fear the woman lived with.

"Who are you?" Sara asked.

"Judi," Mace answered. "My sister."

"Your—" Why would seeing a woman in her brother's embrace frighten Judi so? And why this powerful belief that their paths had crossed before?

"Why?" Judi demanded. She struggled to her feet. "How could you, Mace? How could you?!"

"Sis, stop it!"

"Her!" Judi pointed. "Her! Damn you, damn you!"

Mace didn't move as Judi bolted. The door slammed behind her.

"I'm sorry," Mace said. He didn't try to touch her but leaned against the wall. His hands hung at his sides. He looked like a caged animal that knows there is no escape.

"What is happening?"

He shook his head.

"Would she act like that if she saw you with any woman or is it just me?"

"You," he whispered. His eyes became haunted and as old as his sister's had been.

"I've seen her before," she admitted, "but I can't remember where." Maybe a minute ago she'd been looking forward to fucking Mace. Now she wasn't sure she ever wanted him to touch her again—but why? What was going on? "And she recognized me. Mace, you know, don't you?"

He nodded.

Last night he'd ordered her not to speak, and like a dutiful submissive, she'd obeyed. Now, although she could have begged him to explain, she knew it would do no good.

"What do you think is going to happen?" she demanded. "If you won't tell me what's going on, do you believe I'll forget all about it? That I'm so desperate for sex nothing else matters? You shove your cock in me and I'll become your willing slave? Mindless, pliant the way I was before?"

"You were never that."

He was right, but at the moment she hated her inability to decide what to do. One thing she did know—she couldn't think as long as he stared at her.

"I'm going to go for a walk," she announced. "If you don't want lunch to burn, you'd better turn off the stove. I don't know when I'll be back."

* * * * *

During the drive here, Sara had looked forward to exploring the orchard, but she barely noted her surroundings. At first she'd been in such turmoil she'd been unable to concentrate but walking had calmed her a little. She still didn't understand Judi's reaction or Mace's silence, but those things now seemed part of a melodramatic movie. Had she seen the resemblance between brother and sister and mistakenly assumed she'd met Judi before?

She couldn't let Mace get away with keeping her in the dark. If there was ever going to be anything between them, he *had* to be honest.

Today? Would she demand answers today or wait until they'd fucked?

"You'd like that, wouldn't you?" she muttered. "Why ask for honesty when you can spend your time with your legs spread?"

Or tied closed if that's what Mace wanted.

Last night the image would have excited her, but this was today—reality time. Teeth clenched, she turned her back on the fantasy born of sex in a dark park and started back. She couldn't make herself walk faster but at least she was making progress. Besides, she needed time to decide what she planned to say to him.

* * * * *

Mace wasn't there. He'd turned off the skillet, but although she checked the whole house, she didn't find him. Maybe he'd gone into another part of the orchard.

She found herself back in the bedroom where her suitcase lay on the bed. Mace had opened it but hadn't taken anything out. Was this his subtle way of letting her know he wanted her to stay but was leaving the decision up to her?

Feeling too big for the room, she'd started to turn around when she remembered seeing a manila envelope in his bottom dresser drawer while putting his things away. It had struck her as being out of place among his clothing. She had no right spying on him.

But wouldn't he have kept an ordinary envelope in the small room that served as his office?

The more she thought about it, the uneasier she became. A man living alone had no reason to hide things. If he'd put it there because he didn't dare get rid of it but didn't want to look at it—

Secrets, Mace. How can you keep secrets from me when you know everything about me?

Her hand shook as she opened the drawer and took out the envelope. She sat on the bed and undid the latch, but nearly a minute passed before she took out the contents.

Newspaper clippings.

Frowning, she picked up the top one. As she did, she spotted a sheet of white paper with a photograph in the middle, probably copied from the original.

Suddenly she couldn't breathe. Her heart hammered so it

hurt. Blood rushed to her head, and she felt sick. She didn't need a closer look.

A picture of her. Naked. Arms tied behind her, a collar around her neck. Hair sticking to her sweating throat. Despair haunting her eyes.

"No," she whimpered. "No."

"Sara, what—?"

Feeling as if she might explode, she whirled on Mace. "What are you doing?" she demanded. "Were you hiding, waiting to sneak up on me?"

"No." If anything, his eyes were darker than they'd been earlier. He glanced down at the newspaper clippings, then at her. "I've been checking the irrigation system, but I thought you might have come back. We need—"

"How did you get this?" She snatched up the paper with her picture on it and threw it at him. It fluttered to the floor, photograph up. "Damn it, Mace, how?"

"It was in Ronnie's wallet."

In Ronnie's wallet. Her brain felt overloaded. "Where is the original?"

He started toward her but stopped when she sprang to her feet. "In my wallet," he said.

From her husband's possession to her lover's?

"Why?" Her head felt as if it would split. She pressed her hand to her temple. "Why Mace?"

His fingers closed around her wrists. She needed to fight him, to hate him. Instead, she didn't struggle as he flattened her hands against his chest.

"Because the look in your eyes haunted me, Sara."

"My eyes?" *Not my naked and bound body?*

"Have you seen it before?" he asked.

"I-I stood there while he took it. I had no choice." *Why are you telling him anything?* "I begged him not to, but I knew it

184

wouldn't make any difference."

"I'm so sorry."

With those three words, the fight went out of her, and she sagged against him. "He wanted me to be nothing, his object. He said…he said because he couldn't keep me with him all the time, he deserved pictures to remind him of-of what I was like."

Mace kicked the paper and sent it sliding under the bed. "You weren't an object, Sara. I never saw that."

"What *did* you see?"

"A survivor. A prisoner, one who has experienced the worst but hasn't given up. A fighter."

"I couldn't."

"Not then. But you left him."

"Yes," she admitted and started crying.

"Don't, please. Please, sweetheart."

Feeling weak and strong at the same time, she let him hold her as she cried. She was still sobbing when he started rubbing the small of her back. At first the caress made little impact, but bit-by-bit, the sensation took over, and her pussy responded. She tried to silence it, tried to hold onto the questions she needed to ask, but they melted under his expert manipulation.

She let him sit her on the bed again and accepted the tissue he got from the bathroom, watched him move the newspaper clippings and her suitcase. She'd worn a pullover shirt today and put up no resistance when he drew it off her. Next came her bra. He had her stand while he removed the rest of her clothes, then guided her back onto the bed. Shaking, she watched him undress.

He stared down at her, his expression somber. She looked up at this stranger, this man with his dark secrets. Last night she'd let him place ropes around her and had dreamed of other times and other ways they'd explore that aspect of their

185

relationship. No matter what happened in the future, she'd never forget that last night she'd trusted him in every way.

Not telling him any of those things, she spread her legs and reached for him. After a brief hesitation, he climbed onto the bed and straddled her. His weight bowed the mattress, sinking her into softness. Her slick cunt and hard clit waited for his touch, his control.

With a sigh of surrender, she took hold of his hips and guided him lower. At the same time, she lifted her hips.

"You're sure?" he asked.

"No. But do it now, now."

Sara's innocent and ignorant words took Mace beyond the last of his self-control. Hating himself, he spread her and ran his cock into her hot opening. Although he'd have done anything to wipe away her look of horror when she'd seen the picture, in many ways he was relieved.

She knew at least this much about him.

She became his life, his reason for drawing breath. Despite a nearly overwhelming need to brand her cunt with his cock, he forced himself to be gentle. She'd remember this ride, his kindness and consideration, and his love for the rest of her life.

In his mind, he shifted position and became the one underneath. She might have turned herself over to bondage in the past, but not this time. Today, this moment, they became equals, two hungry and hurting hearts bleeding into each other. With infinite care, he stroked her pussy. He gave her the gift of his cock, his seed, his sweat, but most of all his love.

She kept repeating his name. It became a chant, a cadence, part of both their heartbeats.

"I want this." She sounded as if she was strangling. "I need this." She punctuated her words by grinding her nails into his shoulder blades.

Oblivious to pain, he continued his long and deep strokes. His muscles strained. He dripped sweat. His head felt as if it might blow. Still, he refused to rush his release.

"Mace! Please?"

"What?"

"Do me! Just do me!" She strained toward him and kept opening and closing her legs as much as his body over hers allowed.

She wanted all of him, hard and heavy, yet he somehow found the self-control to continue what felt like a languid pace. He brought her along slow and steady, stroking the ultimate sensation out of her, guiding her minute step by minute step up the mountain.

"Mace!"

Remember my name and this time for the rest of your life.

Her breasts arched toward him, and she threw her head back against the bed and arched her pelvis toward him. But if he rammed into her, it would be over in a flash. Teeth grinding against his screaming need for release, he slipped out of her and leaned back on his heels.

Eyes glazed, she stared up at him. "Mace?"

One second, two, he made her hang suspended over the release they both craved. Then he pushed on her belly, flattening her against the bed. Her knees remained bent. Her weeping pussy hung open to him.

Ignoring himself, he stroked her swollen lips. He dipped into her and came out with juice-flooded fingers. As she watched, he tasted her gift, then went back for more which he deposited on her nipples. She reached for him, but he placed her arms by her side, pressing on her wrists to let her know she was to keep them there. Again he bathed his fingers from her pussy-fountain, then fed her to herself. She lapped greedily, hips moving.

Driven by a force beyond control, he placed his thumb and forefinger at her opening. After guiding them into her as far as he could, he spread them.

She bucked repeatedly and made mewling sounds punctuated by their mutual heavy breathing. Changing direction, he rotated his fingers from side to side as her cunt muscles spasmed. He swore she'd climax before him, but with a growl, she pushed herself off the bed and at him. They tumbled back together, this time with her on top.

"My turn!" she all but screamed. Then she settled herself over him, held his cock in place and buried him in her dark hole. "My turn!"

Driven by her sudden aggression, he did the only thing he could—he accommodated the message in her tightly clamped muscles. She clung to him and imprisoned him with her pussy, drove down and up, down and up. Feeding off her urgent rhythm, he strained and pushed. Their fucking lacked rhythm but what the hell! It felt good, hard and hot and out-of-control. His back burned; maybe it would break. He gripped her arms and pushed her up so she now balanced herself on her knees over him.

She cupped her breasts, then ran her hands down to her nipples and squeezed. When her head sagged back, exposing the long, vulnerable column of her neck, he gripped her thighs and held her against him, imprisoning both of them.

Grunting and cursing by turn, he hammered into her, spending his strength and cum in a violent explosion. He felt her shudder, the tremor radiating out from her cunt until she shook all over. With the last of his strength, he bent himself nearly in half as if doing so would send his cum clear to her breasts.

She twisted from side to side. Sobbed.

Chapter Twenty-Four

ဆ

Sara stared up at Mace who stood with his back to her as he dressed. She felt both beaten and caressed. The mix of sensations left her confused and unable to move.

How had she become a bitch in heat?

Why?

The raging fire began to cool, and although she didn't want it, with sexual satisfaction came sanity. Careful not to let her thoughts go beyond what she was doing, she got off the bed, and picked up the newspaper clippings Mace had brushed to the floor.

Mace, who'd pulled up his jeans but hadn't put on his shirt, turned toward her. If he tried to take the clippings from her, she'd fight him, but he only watched. His eyes turned wary and trapped.

A scan of the headlines told her what she'd feared she'd find. This was the story of Ronnie's murder. She sat on the edge of the bed, oblivious to her naked state, and read. In all, there were five articles and although the material often repeated itself, she was able to pull together a chronology of the last night of her husband's life.

From what detectives had determined from their investigation, Ronnie had left his rig at the truck stop and driven into town, specifically a succession of bars. He'd wound up at the Drink Easy, a hangout popular with office workers. Ronnie hadn't arrived until after midnight when most of the customers had already gone home. Drunk and belligerent because he couldn't get the Drink Easy to accept his out-of-state check, he'd hit on a young waitress who police declined to identify.

According to witnesses, she'd rejected Ronnie's advances and the bar owner had ordered him to leave. When the waitress headed for her car at the end of her shift, she'd found Ronnie waiting for her in the deserted parking lot. He'd jumped her and knocked her to the ground. Then he'd viscously attacked her. According to the waitress, a couple of men came to her rescue. In the confusion, she'd managed to get into her car and speed away.

"The waitress insists she doesn't know the men who stopped the attack. She made it home but apparently passed out once she got inside. Her brother found her and took her to the hospital. She has seen a psychiatrist who expressed concerns for her emotional health. She sustained a concussion, lost several teeth, and had two broken ribs in addition to a dislocated wrist and numerous cuts and bruises."

The report went on to say that the woman was experiencing some traumatic amnesia and had only limited recollection of the attack. Parmenter's body hadn't been discovered until hospital personnel alerted police who interviewed her while she was being treated. Despite a thorough investigation of the crime scene, there were no useful clues leading to the identification of the men involved in Parmenter's death. According to the coroner, he died as a result of multiple stab wounds.

The last article, written a week after Ronnie's death, said detectives were pessimistic about a satisfactory resolution to the murder although they continued to hope that the waitress would remember more about the men who'd come to her rescue. Things finished with a plea by the head detective for anyone who knew anything to come forward.

Although she felt hollowed out, Sara's fingers didn't shake as she dropped the clippings. Mace hadn't moved. "You told me you found his car in an orchard," she whispered. "Why did you lie to me?"

"I didn't think it would matter."

Suddenly aware of how vulnerable she looked with

nothing on, she forced her feet under her. Without a word, she walked into the bathroom and turned on the shower. When the water was hot, she stepped in and let it run over her sensitive flesh. For a long time she simply stood there while the last chapter in Ronnie's life played out in her mind.

"You didn't know how to be gentle, did you?" she whispered. "You had so much anger and violence inside you. When it exploded, you had no control over it." She reached for the shampoo bottle and began washing her hair. "You didn't want to be like that. I saw you with animals and knew you could be gentle, but you lived on the dark side. It controlled you."

For a moment she thought she sensed his presence, then dismissed it. Reading about his murder had brought back memories. Just the same, she wanted to say more to the man she'd married—only, what did it matter? She thought of his cold and lifeless body lying in an oil-stained gravel parking lot and wondered if he'd been conscious as the blood flowed out of him. Had he been afraid? Had he become the lost and frightened little boy he'd once been?

Tears mixed with shampoo and ran off her.

* * * * *

"I want to go there."

"No, you don't."

"If you don't take me, I'll go by myself."

"Why?" Mace demanded.

Ignoring him, she opened her suitcase and got out clean clothes. He'd seen her beyond naked so what did modesty matter? Besides, given her inner turmoil, she could barely concentrate on what she needed to cover her body. She pulled on panties and started in on her bra. She fastened it and spun the hook around to the back but didn't pull the cups over her breasts.

"When the sheriff came and told us Ronnie had been

murdered, all I felt was relief," she told him. "None of us asked for details—protecting Esta I guess and because I felt guilty for wanting him dead. Then you came and told me that lie about finding the car in the orchard, and I thought he'd died near there. Now—" She jerked up on the bra and nodded at the newspaper clippings. "Now I know he died because he'd done something worse than he'd ever done to me. I have—" She positioned her breasts in the cups, noting Mace's focus on what she was doing. "I need closure."

"No you don't. Damn it, Sara, you can't change what happened."

Anguished, she slumped to the bed before her legs gave out. "If I'd stood up to him, if I'd charged him with assault, maybe he wouldn't have hurt that other woman."

"And maybe if you'd had him jailed, he would have been so angry he'd have killed her—or you."

She didn't want logic! She needed to beg the innocent waitress to forgive her. "You don't know what I feel." She pressed her hand over her heart. "That poor, poor woman. I—"

At the look in Mace's eyes, her words died. She stared at him.

"It was your sister, wasn't it?" she said.

* * * * *

Sara didn't know if she'd ever been more afraid.

Mace had begged her not to contact Judi until he could go with her, but when he'd had to troubleshoot a problem with the irrigation system, she'd first paced in the small house, then gone through Mace's address book and found where Judi lived.

She hated going behind his back, but much as he loved and wanted to protect his sister, he didn't understand. She and Judi would find a way through their separate nightmares. Because she knew what Ronnie had been capable of, hopefully she'd help Judi heal. Most of all, she'd beg Judi to forgive her.

Thanks to the map in Mace's desk, she hadn't had much trouble finding the nearly new apartment complex inside a secured fencing system. The neighborhood was upscale, making her wonder if Mace paid his sister's rent. She hated knowing Judi needed to feel safe. After identifying herself to the man at the entrance gate as a friend of Judi's brother, she parked and got out. Quite possibly Judi was at work, but she had to try.

Each condo had a private side patio, and as she walked toward Judi's place, she spotted her through the wrought iron fence. She'd been about to call out when Judi looked up. The book she'd been reading fell to the ground. Sara was afraid the other woman would refuse to talk to her. Instead, she got up and unlatched the gate.

"Mace doesn't know I'm here," Sara said. "I, ah, I know about Ronnie attacking you."

Judi's lips went bloodless but she indicated she wanted Sara to sit in the other lawn chair. Before sitting back down, she picked up her book. "Chemistry. I never thought I could understand chemistry, but there's logic to it. Besides, if I'm going to be a nurse, I need it. I'm starting slow, taking a couple of courses and working part-time."

"A nurse. I'm impressed."

"So am I." Judi's smile was tentative but beautiful. "I've come a long way since...since the attack. Sara, I'm sorry I reacted to seeing you the way I did. I can't tell my brother how to live his life after everything he's done for me. I just wish — it took courage for you to come here."

Judi still looked like a porcelain doll, but Sara felt heartened by the way she met her gaze.

"I wish I'd had more back when it counted," Sara admitted. Then slowly and with occasional tears, she told Judi about her marriage. She kept out the most intimate details of Ronnie's love of bondage and intimidation, instead telling her about the flashes of humanity that had kept Ronnie from being a total monster. For the most part, Judi said nothing, but she hung on every word. Once she went inside for a box of tissues and a couple of glasses of iced tea.

Finally Sara had nothing left to say, except to ask for an apology.

"It isn't your fault," Judi said. "When he started beating me, I was so scared I wet myself. I know what fear feels like."

"But if I'd had him thrown in jail, he might—"

"We can't change the past. Besides, unless the police saw him hurting you, it would have been his word against yours."

Ronnie had thrown that in her face.

"I'm just glad those men came by," Sara admitted. She stared at the ground. "I-I should say I'm sorry Ronnie was killed but—"

An icy breeze slapped Sara's cheeks. Heart pounding, she looked around but of course Ronnie wasn't there.

"Have you remembered any more than you told the police?" she asked because she needed to concentrate on something, anything other than old tapes. "Maybe you don't want to try. I mean, if it had been me, I wouldn't want any memories."

Judi shook her head. Then she leaned forward and took Sara's hand but didn't look up. "Did he tell you?" she asked.

"Mace? Tell me what?"

Judi worried her lower lip. Her grip became stronger. "I haven't said anything to anyone. When he told me, I promised I never would. But you're different."

"What are you talking about?" Had the frigid gust of wind returned? Was that why she felt so cold?

Her head came up. "I—oh God, I don't know if I should— but you said you used to dream he'd died. It's not like you loved Ronnie."

"No, not for a long, long time."

"Then — Sara, it wasn't strangers who saved my life," Judi whispered. "Mace..."

"Mace what?" She could barely get the words out.

"He killed Ronnie. Saved my life."

* * * * *

Sara didn't remember getting into her Jeep. She couldn't say how long she'd been driving aimlessly and might have gone on until she ran out of gas if people hadn't twice honked at her. With a barely formatted plan, she stopped at a convenience store and asked for directions to the Drink Easy. Although the clerk assured her it wasn't hard to find, she begged him to draw her a map.

Feeling sick and spacey, almost mindless, she parked under a mistletoe-invaded tree at one corner of the gravel parking lot behind the bar. She didn't know what she'd expected, something more upscale because it catered to white-collar workers. There were only two other vehicles in the lot, dusty and somewhat shopworn.

Ronnie's lifeblood had spilled onto the ground here. An evil, complex, and tortured man had died here one night while his estranged wife dreamed of freedom.

While you prayed for him to be dead.

"You lied to me, Mace. Why?" she asked, her voice echoing in the enclosed space. Even as she voiced her question, she believed she knew the answer. Would she have fucked her husband's killer if she'd known the truth, would she?

If she'd been Mace, she wouldn't have wanted to take the risk.

"Not good enough, Mace," she whispered. "Not good enough."

A sudden and terrible need slammed into her. It couldn't be and yet, without reason, she needed to fuck and be fucked.

Well, why not? When had she last looked at or even

thought of Mace without wanting him inside her?

Not caring if anyone saw, she unfastened her slacks and pulled them and her panties down so she could get to her pussy. She pushed her middle finger into herself, cupped her palm around her mons, and squeezed, both trapping and caressing the sexual need she now couldn't fathom Mace ever satisfying again.

Mace had saved his sister, but couldn't he have stopped Ronnie without resorting to deadly violence?

In her mind, she began playing out the scenario as she needed it to be. She *saw* Judi walking out to her car, feet dragging after a stressful shift thanks to the obnoxious drunk. Awareness that she wasn't alone came slowly, initially dismissed as a product of her imagination. Still, she picked up her pace, determined to lock herself in her vehicle.

Too late!

A huge, menacing man launched himself at her.

Sara tried to distract herself from the awful image of a near rape and violent beating by fingering her clit. But although her cunt muscles jumped, she knew she couldn't bring herself to climax—not with the nightmare clinging to her.

Ignoring her sexual hunger, she'd pulled her clothes back up and forced herself to get out of the Jeep. The breeze felt hot and smelled of exhaust fumes from the nearby avenue, but she couldn't stop shivering. She felt something clamp over her wrists. Something else encircled her breasts and squeezed. Yet other punishing hands ran between her ass cheeks.

"No!"

Furious at herself for not being able to keep Ronnie out of her mind and body, she whirled in a circle.

Nothing. No one.

Out of the corner of her eye, she spotted a dusty 4-wheel drive pickup entering the parking lot. She tried to tell herself it was simply a thirsty customer, but the deception didn't last long.

Mace had found her.

Although every fiber in her screamed at her to run, she didn't. She'd done enough running in her life.

He parked nearby, got out, and leaned against the truck door. His stance reminded her of when they'd used a hood and fender to fuck.

"Judi called me," he said.

"Why didn't you tell me?" she demanded.

He didn't answer, merely shook his head.

Staring into his eyes and remembering what his naked and aroused body looked and felt like, she knew she could never hate him. As for trust—

"She's really better?" she asked. "She needs to feel safe but she's going to school."

"Small steps," he told her. "She lived with me for several months after the attack. That's why—part of why—it took me so long to come to you."

But you did because you were obsessed by that damn photograph.

She swallowed. Another frozen wave glided over her skin. She clenched her fist and for a moment—like the trapped animal she'd once been—she tested her surroundings for danger.

"What is it?"

She shook her head and forced herself to dismiss the cold. "You showed your sister that photo of me tied and at his mercy, didn't you? Why?"

"I'm sorry. I didn't want... So she'd understand what kind of man he'd been."

It made sense and yet— "Was that the only reason?"

"No," he admitted after a long silence. "I talked about going to see you; I couldn't get you out of my mind." His gaze slid from her eyes down her body, then up again.

Sexually alive once again, she fought for control by squeezing her thighs together. He must know what she felt, but did it matter?

"She understood, I think. She talked about our needing to know how you were, but she also wanted to put everything behind her, not stirring up memories, or risking detectives reopening the case."

"It's closed?"

He shrugged. "They told me it wasn't a high priority. They'd done some checking of places he went through on his route. He'd come onto women before, roughed several up. One of the detectives said Ronnie looked like a man who had it coming to him. When I admitted I wasn't sure Judi was strong enough for a trial, they agreed."

"Oh."

"Also." Slow and measured, he decreased the distance between them. "I didn't want you drawn into things more than you'd already been."

She managed to keep herself under control until he touched her. At the brush of finger against the side of her neck, she shuddered and jumped away. He'd murdered her husband and lied about it.

Chapter Twenty-Five

☙

She'd expected the bar's interior to be dark, but bright lights revealed it for what it was—a run-of-the-mill bar in the middle of the day with a middle-aged man running a vacuum cleaner over a shopworn carpet.

The man had told her and Mace that they wouldn't open for another hour, but Mace had said he simply wanted to show it to her, and they'd leave in a few minutes.

In truth, she'd been the one who'd insisted on coming in. She hadn't been able to explain why since Ronnie had died outside, but now as she looked around, she knew.

Unable to control her trembling, she took in her surroundings. Mace stood nearby.

Bits and pieces of the nightmare that had haunted her since Ronnie's death returned. She placed her hands on the bar and stared into the mirror, not seeing shattered glass as she had in her dreams but her and Mace's reflections.

"I feel bodies," she whispered, unable to take her eyes off her haunted expression. "Smell smoke. The bar is crowded, people laughing. I'm watching and afraid although I don't know why. Maybe I feel the woman's fear."

"My sister's?"

She nodded. "In my dream, I'm angry at those people for not doing anything to help her. Then...then everything shifts and I'm outside. So are the woman and her attacker—Judi and Ronnie."

"Don't do this, Sara," Mace begged.

"I have to. Otherwise, it's never going to be finished." *Otherwise I won't know if I can forgive you – or myself.*

Something else was propelling her into the nightmare, but she lacked the courage to voice her fear. Instead, she concentrated on what she needed to do—marrying dream and reality so finally she'd know everything.

She stared into the mirror but didn't really see it. Maybe she should go back outside, but she believed the dream was powerful enough to play itself out where everything had begun.

"Now we're outside," she continued. She felt Mace's presence—and something else. "Ronnie looks huge to Judi, massive. She screams and tries to run, but she can't get away. He loves his control, tormenting her. He's drunk but not so drunk he doesn't know what he's doing. He smells her helplessness." She closed her eyes briefly, then continued the unwanted but necessary journey.

"He wants her terrified and although he can hardly wait to rape her, he tries to draw things out. She's backing away from him, tripping, falling."

"No."

Suddenly aware of how hard this must be for Mace, she gripped his hand. "I'm sorry. If you don't want me to—"

"No. I need to know."

Need to know? But he'd been there, hadn't he?

Determined to go on, she plunged back into night. "She hates his laughter, and she hates her helplessness. Terror is in her throat and between her breasts. But she's also angry. H-he calls her a cunt, and she spits at him."

"Good."

Sara didn't care if the man with the vacuum cleaner was watching. "She tries to stand, but he straddles her."

"Judi's blouse had been torn off."

"Yes." She wanted to make this part as easy for Mace as possible. "He does that while she's on the ground. Then he lets her get up. She's screaming but there's no one to hear—except you. When did you—?"

"Enough, Sara."

No, not enough, cunt. Ride this one to the end.

"Ronnie," she managed.

Mace pulled her against him, his grip unrelenting. "What about Ronnie?"

"Nothing." *Go away! Leave! You're dead!* "She, ah, Judi is on her feet again, but he's gotten hold of her keys so she can't use her car to get away. She tries to run, but he starts hitting her. He slaps her face, her breasts, then punches her repeatedly. She's—I don't want to tell you this."

"I don't want to hear it, but we both have to."

How horribly right he was.

"She's crying and begging him not to hurt her. She says she won't fight any more and will do whatever he wants as long as he stops hitting her. Sh-she hates herself for saying those things, but she can't help it. She'll do whatever it takes to go on living."

Mace turned her toward him and hugged her to his chest. "Just like you did," he whispered.

Yes. "She can't get him to listen because he's getting off on punishment. She wants to be dead and prays her brother will come in time."

Mace's arms spasmed, but he didn't release her. His breathing turned ragged.

She plunged back into the nightmare.

"She has something in her hand. She can barely hold onto it, but she knows that without it, she's dead. He stops for a moment because he's been drinking so much his stomach is upset. Grabbing hold of every bit of courage and strength left in her, she—she plunges her knife into Ronnie's belly."

Drained, Sara leaned back so she could stare into Mace's eyes.

"He's still standing so she pulls it out and stabs him

201

again. Over and over again."

* * * * *

"You lied for your sister, didn't you?" Sara said.

Mace nodded.

"Because you were afraid knowing she was a murderer was more than she could handle."

"She'd been through enough. Sara, do you want to know more?"

They'd left the bar and were back in the parking lot. The graveled area felt cut apart from civilization. Except for their vehicles and the two belonging to the employees, they had it to themselves.

"Yes," she told him.

He took her hands and rested them on his chest. "The owner had called me about the drunk who'd hit on Judi so I decided to show up at quitting time. I was late. Damn it, I was late. I found her unconscious next to Ronnie's body. I wasn't thinking straight. All I wanted to do was protect my sister."

As she took in Mace's heartbeat through her fingers, he told her about bundling Judi in his car and driving her home. She came around but babbled incoherently. He called his foreman and between them they came up with a plan to try to protect Judi. It wasn't perfect, a lathered plot pulled together by two shocked but determined men. Mace had given his sister a double dose of sleeping pills and he and Hugo had driven back to the bar.

To their relief, nothing had changed. They'd hidden Ronnie's vehicle in the orchard, then driven Judi's car home. They'd also taken Ronnie's wallet, thinking it would look as if someone had robbed Ronnie and taken his car after killing him.

On their way to the hospital, Mace had taken advantage of Judi's amnesia by telling her he'd killed Ronnie to save her.

She was to tell detectives she remembered several men stopping the attack, then climbing in her car and speeding away.

"The plan had so many holes in it, so many things I wasn't sure were going to hold up. But the doctors say Judi will probably never remember what happened. I bought her silence with a lie. She'd do anything to protect me."

Sara's mind spun, not just from what Mace had told her but because she knew beyond all doubt that they weren't alone.

Chapter Twenty-Six

ಬಂ

Sara drove back to Mace's house while he followed close behind. She'd said nothing to him before getting into her car and now walked inside without a word. She went into the bedroom and closed the door behind her because she needed to put space between her and this life-changing man.

Even more she needed to come to terms with Ronnie.

Because she had no choice, she lay on the bed and closed her eyes. *Come to me*, she told her former husband. *Once and for all, let's have this out.*

He killed me.

No, he didn't, Ronnie, you know it. Judi—she was trying to save herself. She believed you were going to kill her. If it had been me, I'd have done the same thing.

When he didn't respond, she spoke aloud. "Ronnie, no matter what you do, it won't change reality. You're still dead. You'll never fuck another woman, never touch one, not really and not beyond my dreams—my nightmares. Go—where you belong."

I'll take you with me!

Although his threat made her shiver, she refused to back down. "Even if you can, nothing will change. I'll never want what passed for fucking between us."

In her mind's eye, a scene began developing. She *saw* herself walking naked between rows of almond trees. Her steps seemed awkward, forcing her to look closer. No wonder. Ropes were tied around her ankles, giving her barely enough freedom to move.

Now she stood beside her other self, feeling cool air on

her naked body. The same kind of ropes lashing her legs together held her arms behind her. Whoever had done the tying—as if there was any doubt—had wrapped more lengths around her waist and used that to hold her captured wrists high against the small of her back in a way that thrust her breasts out. A broad leather strap tightly gagged her. Other straps on either side of the strip in her mouth came together over her head and fastened to the leather at the back of her head. Momentarily detached from what was happening, she admired the contraption.

Then she felt *his* hands on her breast and hips.

Walk, bitch. Walk until I tell you to stop.

She longed to curse him, but of course she couldn't speak. Her hair had fallen over her eyes, hindering her ability to glare at him. He pushed her from behind, forcing her to stumble forward. She must not be moving fast enough because he grabbed the waist rope and hauled her behind him as he trotted down the endless row.

He was taking her far from Mace—to the nightmare world he lived in.

Knowing nothing except that she wouldn't go without a fight, she dug in and brought them both to a halt.

You know where we're going, bitch. To where I can always do what I want with you.

No!

Fury, not fear, filled her. Leaning back, she yanked free, then turned and stumbled into the trees. She'd reached the first one when he threw himself against her and knocked them both to the ground. She lay under him, his weight and strength defeating her.

He'd take her to his hell. Keep her there forever.

Mace, Mace!

Don't say his name, Ronnie warned. *Don't even think it!*

He gave weight to his words by pushing off her. Before

she could give thought to resistance, he straddled her waist so he'd ground her belly and breasts into the weeds and dirt. He patted her ass, then roughly kneaded her buttocks, laughing when she squirmed and cursed and drooled under the painful gag.

He stopped kneading, and she felt him do something to the rope at her waist. He leaned over her, pressing one hand against the back of her thigh, and snagged the ankle tether. Laughing, he yanked, forcing her to bend her knees so her heels touched her ass. Although she twisted and turned under him, it did no good. He easily hogtied her, using the short length of rope he'd added to the loops around her waist.

Getting off her, he rolled her onto her side. *Look at that, all done up like a Christmas gift.* His tone sobered. *I'll never have another Christmas, Sara. You took it from me.*

Don't blame me! You're responsible —

He knelt beside her and gently stroked her breasts, belly, hips, thighs, between her legs.

It doesn't have to be like this, Sara. I can be gentle. He forced her knees apart and ran a finger in her pussy. *See what I mean, gentle.*

It was. Despite her helpless moan, this touch brought no pain — and no pleasure.

Weep, for me, Sara. Let your pussy cry for me.

It remained dry.

No! He sounded like a lost child. *No, Sara, this is my playground.* He pushed further. *I can make it my playground, I can!*

His finger rasped against her barren inner walls. He kept at her, stroking and teasing. In the past, her sexuality had betrayed her, but now she had nothing to give him.

Bitch! *Whore*! He gave her one more desperate stroke, then pulled out. He looked at her body as if he hated it, burning her with a glare she'd never seen before. In the past, no matter what he'd done to her, there'd been a sense of awe about his manipulations as if he didn't believe she belonged to him. Now, she had no doubt. He loathed her.

I loathe you too, she told him in the only way he'd left her. *I'm glad you're dead. I hope it took a long time, and you tasted fear until your last breath.*

Cursing, he rolled her away from him. Her right breast ground into a rock. He slid his hand under the leather at the back of her head as he tied yet more of the endless rope to it. He yanked, forcing her to arch her head back and exposing her throat. She felt him tie this new rope to her waist bondage.

You think I can't control you? he asked. He spread his hand over her throat and squeezed. *How's that bitch, how's that?*

Mace, Mace, Mace!

Stop it! You'll never speak his name again, never!

She could barely breathe as once again he rolled her onto her side. He let her see as he pulled yet more rope out of his pocket. This too he tied to her waist but in front this time. Then he ran the length between her legs, snagged it against her cunt, and secured it by finishing the tie at her wrists.

Got your attention, bitch? Tight enough for you, bitch?

Mace, Mace, Mace.

He studied her for a moment with a puzzled expression. Then he smiled. *Nearly done but not quite. One thing about where I am...* He produced still more rope. *I have access to all kinds of toys.*

Although he'd already stripped her of all ability to move, he wrapped the rope around and around her thighs, lashing them tightly together. *Do you get it?* he asked when he'd finished. *If I can't have access to your pussy, neither can you. Maybe I'll keep it – and you – like that forever.* He tugged on the rope between her legs. *Pussy's not much good to you this way, is it?*

To her horror, he leaned close and positioned his teeth just above her throat. *I can suck the life out of you, Sara. End you.*

Do it. Do it! Then I'll never belong to you!

I'll bring you with me.

I don't belong in your hell. Only you live there, only you.

He opened his mouth wide, but instead of biting her neck, he bathed it with his tongue. At the same time, he caressed her cheeks, forehead, nose, eyelids, even ran his fingers over her ears.

I can be gentle, Sara, he said softly. *Don't you see, I can make you love me?*

Never!

Looking hurt, he tried to slide his hand between her legs, but he'd tied her too tightly. *Are you wet? Please, Sara, are you wet yet?*

Never.

Don't say that, please.

Please. How rare the word was coming from him. Understanding as she'd never understood anything in her life, she focused all her will on this one thing.

I feel sorry for you, Ronnie. I don't know if you believe me, but I do. You never had a chance – not the way someone abandoned you as an infant. You didn't receive love when it mattered most so you didn't learn how to give. No matter what you do to me, it won't change the way I feel.

Love me, Sara, please, love me.

I can't. I love Mace. He has my heart, my body, my everything.

She thought Ronnie might laugh because he owned her physical body in every possible way, but he didn't. Instead, he shifted position so she could look at him. Warm drops landed on her breast, and she heard Ronnie's ragged breath.

I hurt for you, Ronnie. I wish your life could have been different – that you and I could have been different. But it'll never be. Let me go. Find peace, somehow.

Another of his tears ran off her nipple, but she hardened herself to him. No one had forced him to do the things he had. Only he could have changed – not the two decent people who'd tried to parent him and not her. She sensed him trying to break through her barriers and force her to listen to him, to believe his tears.

Mace, Mace, I love you. You've shown me what it is to be a woman, to love my body and mind. I want you in my life — not need because I can go on alone if I have to, but want. I feel complete around you, in love and loved.

Her mind divorced her from her body and the man who'd worked so hard to claim it. Only one thing existed — Mace's touch, Mace's embrace. Mace's cock housed in her.

Because of you I embrace both sunlight and night. I left a barren land and came with you to a place filled with rich earth and growing things. I want to grow flowers for you, for us to smell them together, to make love in the moonlight, have sex on your bed, fuck in this orchard.

Flashes of red and orange filled her vision. Ronnie had made it impossible for her to move her head so she could only wait — and listen.

Now she heard male voices. Ronnie's was filled with rage but lacked the strength she'd always associated with it. Instead, he whispered, as if his throat was closing down.

In contrast, Mace spoke with command and compassion, his tone unwavering. She didn't understand the words. It was as if they were communicating on a level beyond speech, one composed of emotion alone.

Then she sensed movement and waited for the battle to begin.

Instead, familiar hands touched her throat. Out of the corner of her eye, she spotted a beloved face. Beyond him she saw trees. She smelled earth and growing things.

"I love you," Mace said. He bent over her and kissed her cheek, then cut through the rope at the back of her head. She sucked in her first deep breath since Ronnie had imprisoned her.

Mace kissed her again and removed the gag.

"I love you," she told him through dry lips.

"I'm sorry. I didn't want to wait, but I knew you and Ronnie—"

"You saw?"

He nodded. Embarrassment flashed through her but faded as Mace removed the rest of her bonds. Holding her against him, he massaged the tension out of her shoulders and thighs.

"I wanted to come into the bedroom. You'll never know how much," he said. "But I knew you needed time alone. The phone rang in my office. I went to answer it, but no one was there. By the time I returned, the bedroom and front doors were open, and you were gone."

She glanced at the marks on her wrists and ankles then turned her attention to Mace. He touched her everywhere except her breasts and pubic area. Although she hadn't seen Ronnie since the discussion between him and Mace had begun, she still sensed his presence. "He's here," she said.

"I know. I told him he'd had his time with you while I was looking for you. Now it's my turn."

My turn.

She'd never been more sure of anything as she took Mace's hands and placed them over her breasts." Do you see this, Ronnie?" she asked. "I want this."

Their surroundings darkened.

"Ronnie, my body is a gift I give freely to the man I love." She arched her breasts toward Mace and moaned under his gentle massage.

The darkness came closer.

"In every way a woman can give herself to a man, I give myself to Mace." She slipped out of Mace's arms and repositioned herself so she lay on her back. She bent her knees and opened her legs, her cunt to Mace. "I trust this man," she said as her opening heated. "Do you see, Ronnie? You couldn't make me wet, couldn't force me to accept you. It's different now — in every way."

Eyes on Mace and mouth open, she inched closer and spread her legs even more. Lifting her buttocks off the ground, she waited.

Mace slid his hands up the inside of her thighs, spread her lips and used his fingers to ease liquid heat out of her. "See it, Ronnie," he said. "Smell her."

No!

"Yes," Sara and Mace said at the same time.

Mace left her long enough to strip off his clothes. Returning, he knelt before her offered pussy, then positioned her legs around his hips, lifted her onto his thighs and kissed his cock to her opening.

"I'm taking him," she said. "Willingly, gladly. His cock is his gift to me."

"Her hot cunt and hard, swollen clit proof of her trust," Mace said.

He slammed into her, the penetration smooth and complete, a wedding of male and female sex organs. She fell back on the ground and caressed what she could reach of his thighs as Mace, her lover, her man, took her.

She felt as if she was swimming in a liquid world. Nothing of her recent imprisonment lingered on her body or in her mind, and she became new, a virgin.

Then Mace's strokes turned hard and honest and she turned into a whore. A whore fucking with body, mind, and soul.

Her climax slammed into her, surprising her with its quickness. Her legs turned into jelly but her pussy — her pussy contracted and expanded by dizzying turn. She used her powerful cunt muscles to hold Mace's cock inside her as he pushed, pushed again, grunted.

His cum washed her pussy, extending her climax, filling

her, marrying her to him.

"I love you, love you!" she sobbed.

"I love you, love you." His climax arched his back and briefly silenced him. "I love you," he whispered when he could speak.

Her vision cleared. The day was bright, the air light.

"He's gone," they said.

Epilogue

&

"I'm home."

"The conquering hero returns?"

"Heroine." Sara laughed. "Women are heroines."

"Duly noted," Mace said and got up from his desk. He nodded, indicating he'd noticed that she kept both hands behind her back. "So, how did it go?"

"Good. Great." She'd wanted to draw out the suspense but couldn't hide her smile. "I was so afraid I'd forgotten how to study. Wanna see?"

At his enthusiastic nod, she handed him the paper with the grade from her first biology test on it. "An A," he said after looking at it. "What else are you hiding?"

"I'll show you in a minute. I swear, you have no patience. I'm lucky you've left me alone long enough for me to study and go to my classes."

"I haven't heard you complain."

"Not so far." Just thinking about what she knew would happen tonight caused her nipples to harden and her belly to tighten. "I talked to Judi afterward. She got a B."

"Is she happy with her grade?"

"I think so. It feels good to talk to her about ordinary things."

"I'm glad, especially since you're taking the same class. Well, woman, are you going to go on standing there? I'd like to get onto the business of congratulating you."

"Hmm." She tightened her thigh muscles, not that it lessened her interest in fucking. "What did you have in mind?"

"Oh." His gaze slid down her body. "I think you know."

"It isn't night. Remember our pact, no sex during daylight hours. Otherwise, we won't get else anything done."

"And how many times have we broken our rule?"

"A lot. Speaking of—" With a flourish, she produced the bag holding the purchase she'd made on the way home. "I've been thinking." She opened the bag and peered in it. "Your place is a male domain."

"I haven't heard you complain."

"I haven't. Besides, we're starting to make improvements." She indicated the new curtains. "But you can't argue that it's a masculine bedroom."

"Yeah, it is."

"So I've been thinking—what's your opinion of yellow?"

He looked suspicious. "Yellow?"

"You know, yellow walls, maybe a pink bedspread with flowers, lacy throw pillows."

"I hope you're kidding."

"Mace, your sheets—blue and brown—give me a break."

"You don't seem opposed to messing them up."

"I'm not, I'm not." She peeked in the bag again and gave him a demure smile. "But you only have two sets and, you know, one set is always in the wash. What do you think of pink and yellow together? Daisies. At least I think they're daisies."

He gave her a *please tell me you're joking* look which only increased her enjoyment. "If we're going to get married—we are tying the knot aren't we?"

"Next weekend."

"Oh yes, next weekend. I knew there was something I had to do." Just thinking about the planned honeymoon to the coast had her all hot and bothered. "Anyway, since we're getting married, I've decided I have every right to exert my influence in the bedroom."

"When haven't you?" He reached for her, but she backed out of reach.

"Good point," she conceded. "But there's more to a woman's bedroom influence than helping a man get rid of his hard-on. There's a matter of flowers and pastels."

Making sure she had Mace's full attention, she pulled the sheet set out of the bag.

"Red," he whispered, eyes widening.

"Deep, rich red." She tore off the plastic wrapping and shook out the sheets and matching pillowcases. "Silk."

"Silk?"

"You don't like?"

"I don't know. I've never—"

"Then why don't we take them on their maiden voyage?" she suggested and threw the sheets over his head.

By the time he'd disengaged himself, she'd run into the bedroom. He stalked toward her, holding the top sheet as if it was a net and he a fisherman. He tossed; she didn't duck.

"Ha, got you, woman," he announced as he threw her, tangled in the sheets, onto the bed. "Come out, come out, I have something to show you."

He indeed did.

Enjoy an excerpt from:
HARD BODIES

Chapter One

෩

He lay on his back, powerful legs straddling the narrow bench, thighs and crotch exposed; he was the next thing to naked. *This is what I am,* his body language said. *Take it or leave it.* Not that any woman alive could ignore that prime piece of meat.

Brandy Schuller couldn't take her eyes off his massive chest and arms, couldn't think beyond the strength exuding from him. Dressed in a skin-tight, sleeveless muscle shirt and nylon shorts that barely contained his thighs and the bulge that fairly screamed *cock*, he looked more than human.

Licking her lips, Brandy leaned against the wall and stared at Franko Priest. The longer she studied the awesome mass of him, the more her skin hummed. No wonder. His muscles were his trademark, the way he supported himself, his in-your-face message to the world. As for *why* she couldn't stop thinking about straddling him and begging him to impale her, well, chalk that up to insanity.

He remained as motionless as he'd been when she walked into the unnervingly empty gym. He held weighted dumbbells at chest level in preparation for a lift, his taut arm muscles looking in as superb condition as the rest of him.

Hard rock music blared throughout the large, well-equipped facility, but at a few minutes past midnight, she and Priest were the only people in the building. Although she'd known it would just be the two of them, unexpected nervousness slid through her. Her gaze remained on the man who'd shattered several world weight-lifting records. Priest, only Priest could help her.

If he didn't scare her to death first.

Slow and steady, he began pushing the dumbbells into the air. The pectoral muscles across his upper chest contracted, as did his triceps. They grew larger, expanding to impossible proportions. What sane woman would dare crawl on top of him? What insane one wouldn't fantasize? Well, she admitted, it wasn't the first time she'd had those thoughts when it came to Priest.

The dumbbell chest press was a deceptively simple movement—weights up as far as the arms could extend, then down. He completed one rep and without resting, began another. He could do the same to her, lift her over him, then bring her down, down until he'd buried his cock in her heated pussy.

Oh brother; you are getting carried away tonight, aren't you?

He seemed to have pulled deep inside himself and become nothing more than muscle, bone, and nerves. She'd seen larger men on the posters that decorated the gym walls, but she certainly hadn't seen a more total package in the flesh. She figured his height at around six foot four, and someone had told her that he weighed just under three hundred pounds.

Three hundred pounds! On an ordinary mortal, that would be fat. But everything about Priest shouted muscle. Muscle she'd be spending the next hour with...unless she chickened out.

No! No turning and running; she'd come too far.

Five reps now, pecs knotting and hard as rock. Features contorted, he grunted through the sixth lift, paused a millisecond longer than before, then surged into number seven. She counted with him, felt her own muscles burn and tremble. Her pussy seemed to liquefy, although with anticipation or fear she couldn't say.

Eight. Nine. Ten. Halfway through the eleventh upward movement, he bellowed. The weights thudded to the rubberized mat under the bench, just missing him.

He lay there as if assessing his body. Watching him run a hand over his upper arm, she swore she could feel his sweat-slickened flesh. Beyond all sanity, she imagined her fingers on him, absorbing his heat and raw power.

Franko Priest had been a professional football player who now devoted himself to weight-lifting and bodybuilding. In addition, no one in this part of the state knew more about how the human body worked…how to push it to the edge and beyond. She'd come here for that. Only that.

He sat up, muscles rolling and bunching. He had a football player's thick neck and impossibly wide shoulders. The photographs of him posing during a competition didn't do him justice. Not even his reputation, spoken in awed tones by lesser mortals, had prepared her for her first look at him three months ago. Since then she'd learned that although he took physical conditioning seriously, he didn't expect perfection from those who came to him for advice, thank goodness. She couldn't guess at his percentage of body fat, but there seemed to be nothing except skin over his muscles. Was he soft anywhere?

Maybe his cock when it wasn't erect.

"Have you seen enough, Ms. Schuller?"

She winced and took an unconscious step back. Unfortunately, the wall had no give to it. "Sorry," she muttered. I didn't mean to distract you."

He slid off the bench and stood up, a confident jungle cat. His long, steel-like legs ate up the space separating them, and his mouth lifted in what might become a smile given half a chance. Above that was a long, narrow nose and deep-set chocolate eyes.

He was huge, larger up close than she'd expected! She had to crane her neck to meet his gaze. How that flimsy shirt managed to at least marginally control his sculptured chest she didn't know. His shorts were rolled up over his thighs, further accenting his minimally sheathed cock and balls.

"I could use a distraction," he said. "The truth is, I was getting bored, and I don't dare max out if I don't have a spotter. What do you think of what you saw?"

She swallowed and tried not to breathe in the smell of his sweat. "Impressive lift."

Chuckling, he clenched his fists and struck a classic pose. His muscles expanded even more. His veins looked like garden-hoses snaking just under the skin. "I'm glad you think so. I've certainly had enough practice."

It was her turn to speak; unfortunately, her throat contacted. He folded his arms across his chest...not that they actually folded...and looked down at her. "All right," he said. "We need to get started. First, how honest do you want me to be?"

I don't know. "Honest. Completely."

"All right then. To begin, your breasts are too big."

"What?" she gasped.

"Your breasts are too large."

"They're mine, all mine if that's what you're getting at." She gave a half thought to slapping him. This was hardly the way she'd expected their first session to begin.

"Back up, Brandy. This is an objective assessment, not a come-on."

Not sure she was relieved or disappointed; she struggled not to look down at herself. Priest had told her to meet him at this ungodly hour because it was the only time he had free. In the three months she'd been coming to the gym, she'd come to respect his expertise, and he came highly recommended. Besides, whenever he saw her, he spoke to her, about nothing more earth-shattering than the weather or to offer a suggestion about how to target a particular muscle during an exercise which allowed her to consider him a casual friend. Never before had it been just the two of them.

But after everything she'd been through this year, she wasn't about to turn tail and run.

"Let's begin by clarifying what you want to get out of this," he continued. "Otherwise, I'm not going to be able to give you what you need." He leaned forward and rested his hands on the wall behind her. She was trapped, his muscle-padded chest brushing her breasts with his every breath. "Also, I need to be as efficient as possible with my time. In addition to being the pro here and staying in shape for competitions, I work with the college's athletic department."

"I know," she said, glad to have that to talk about. "I've heard you and some of the other guys discussing the football team. Look, if you're trying to tell me you don't have the time…"

"No. That's not what I'm saying. I'm making a commitment to you because…because I heard you'd been badly hurt last year."

He knew that about her? "I'm not sure," she stammered, suddenly off balance. In addition to feeling exposed and vulnerable, she also felt as if she was becoming part of him, as if her own flesh and sorry muscles were melting into him. Her hands hung by her sides. It was all she could do not to cup them around his cock.

"What aren't you sure about?"

If he guessed what had distracted her…"I may have made a mistake. I have so much to learn. You've seen me blundering around on the equipment. I should start with someone less…"

He was becoming aroused. She sensed rather than saw his cock swell.

"I should have known that was going to happen." He looked down at himself, then shrugged. "A good workout affects everything."

She'd never heard that but wasn't about to call him on it. Neither did she want to discuss his condition.

"Listen to me, Brandy." He'd been keeping a minimum amount of separation between them, but now he let himself sag forward so the tip of his cock poked her belly.

"Bodybuilding is physical. I accepted that a long time ago. You need to too."

Suddenly angry, or maybe dangerously close to letting him know he was turning her on, she dropped down and slipped out from under him.

He turned toward her. To her shock, heat built in her cunt, and she felt heavy between her legs.

"What is this about?" she demanded. "I'm paying good money for some professional advice. That's all I want, not...not this." She indicated his penis.

"I'm not going to apologize for a normal male reaction. Besides, I don't believe it turns you off. In fact..." His mouth twitched. "Unless I'm not reading you correctly, *off* is hardly what you're feeling. Correct?"

Why an electronic book?

We live in the Information Age — an exciting time in the history of human civilization, in which technology rules supreme and continues to progress in leaps and bounds every minute of every day. For a multitude of reasons, more and more avid literary fans are opting to purchase e-books instead of paper books. The question from those not yet initiated into the world of electronic reading is simply: *Why?*

1. *Price.* An electronic title at Ellora's Cave Publishing and Cerridwen Press runs anywhere from 40% to 75% less than the cover price of the exact same title in paperback format. Why? Basic mathematics and cost. It is less expensive to publish an e-book (no paper and printing, no warehousing and shipping) than it is to publish a paperback, so the savings are passed along to the consumer.

2. *Space.* Running out of room in your house for your books? That is one worry you will never have with electronic books. For a low one-time cost, you can purchase a handheld device specifically designed for e-reading. Many e-readers have large, convenient screens for viewing. Better yet, hundreds of titles can be stored within your new library — on a single microchip. There are a variety of e-readers from different manufacturers. You can also read e-books on your PC or laptop computer. (Please note that Ellora's Cave does not endorse any specific brands.

You can check our websites at www.ellorascave.com or www.cerridwenpress.com for information we make available to new consumers.)

3. *Mobility.* Because your new e-library consists of only a microchip within a small, easily transportable e-reader, your entire cache of books can be taken with you wherever you go.

4. **Personal Viewing Preferences.** Are the words you are currently reading too small? Too large? Too… ANNOYING? Paperback books cannot be modified according to personal preferences, but e-books can.

5. **Instant Gratification.** Is it the middle of the night and all the bookstores near you are closed? Are you tired of waiting days, sometimes weeks, for bookstores to ship the novels you bought? Ellora's Cave Publishing sells instantaneous downloads twenty-four hours a day, seven days a week, every day of the year. Our webstore is never closed. Our e-book delivery system is 100% automated, meaning your order is filled as soon as you pay for it.

Those are a few of the top reasons why electronic books are replacing paperbacks for many avid readers.

As always, Ellora's Cave and Cerridwen Press welcome your questions and comments. We invite you to email us at Comments@ellorascave.com or write to us directly at Ellora's Cave Publishing Inc., 1056 Home Avenue, Akron, OH 44310-3502.

COMING TO A BOOKSTORE NEAR YOU!

ELLORA'S CAVE

Bestselling Authors Tour

UPDATES AVAILABLE AT
WWW.ELLORASCAVE.COM

Cerridwen, the Celtic Goddess of wisdom, was the muse who brought inspiration to story-tellers and those in the creative arts. Cerridwen Press encompasses the best and most innovative stories in all genres of today's fiction. Visit our site and discover the newest titles by talented authors who still get inspired - much like the ancient storytellers did, once upon a time.

Cerridwen Press

www.cerridwenpress.com